CW00819729

Once in a Blue Moon

Miranda Twist

Illustrated by Karen Donnelly

Some of the characters lurking inside this book.

The awesome yo yitsoo

A troll

A pelican fox

Be prepared for a story where magic goes terribly wrong!

Once in a Blue Moon

MIRANDA TWIST

Published in the UK by Everything with Words Limited
3rd Floor, Premier House,
12-13 Hatton Garden, London EC1N 8AN

www.everythingwithwords.com

Text copyright © Miranda Twist 2017
Illustrations copyright © Karen Donnelly 2017

Miranda Twist has asserted her right under the Copyright, Design and
Patents Act 1988 to be identified as the author of this work.

This books is sold subject to the condition that it shall not, by way of
trade or otherwise, be lent, resold, hired out, or otherwise circulated
without the publisher's prior consent in any form of binding or cover
other than that in which it is published and without a similar condition,
including this condition, being imposed on the subsequent purchaser.

ISBN 978-1-911427-01-8

Printed and bound in Great Britain by Clays Ltd, St Ives plc

To anyone who's ever experienced
bad magic and survived.

To all you who's ever experienced

being here and survived.

The Wood

The boy and his sister lived in a house with a small garden at the front and a bigger one at the back. It wasn't much bigger but it was special because behind it was a wood. The wood was huge. In winter the trees held out their bare branches like the hands of many-fingered giants and when the wind blew there was a strange sound. In summer it was difficult to see how big it really was, but it looked like the sort of place you could really get lost. Yes, it was humongous. And it was right behind their garden— it couldn't have been closer. Sometimes the boy and the girl would look out of their bedroom window at the wood.

'That wood is creepy,' the girl used to say.

'That wood is full of magic,' the boy would reply.

He said that even when he knew she would get

angry. 'What rubbish you're talking. What awe-some, weird and terrible rubbish you are talking. One day the garingay are going to get you.'

His sister was called Lucy and she was almost always right. He was called Henry and he was almost always wrong. He didn't know why. It just seemed to happen. Somehow he was always saying things that couldn't be true. He didn't mean to. The things just popped into his head and felt true. They felt so true that he had to say them even when he knew that no one would believe him.

'The wood is full of magic and trolls.'

'What rubbery rubbish you're talking—and what big lies. What ginormous lies. The garingay will get you.'

'The garingay?'

'The garingay eat little boys. They eat them for breakfast. They like them because they are smelly and chewy.'

The boy looked at his sister. He couldn't believe what he was hearing.

'You are talking rot and rhubarb. The sort of stuff people say to babies, just to scare them to pieces because they'll believe anything. There is no such thing as garingay.'

'Well, if there are trolls…'

'There are trolls,' said Henry very quietly, in that voice he used when he was being serious and knew what he was talking about. That voice would drive Lucy mad. It would drive her so mad that she would slam doors, stamp and stick her tongue out.

'There aren't any trolls,' she stamped. 'There are no trolls.' She stuck her tongue out. 'No trolls. Ever.'

He heard the slam of the door and her steps on the stairs.

He looked down at his feet and there it was. He knew immediately what it was: a very small troll and just possibly the smallest troll in the whole world. And it was looking at him with those big round troll eyes.

'This is my garden,' said the troll in a voice so deep that it seemed to be coming from somewhere in the ground.

'It is,' repeated the troll in his deep mellow voice. 'It really, really is my garden. Why, this is my dog and I'm taking my dog for a walk in my garden. I wouldn't take it for a walk in some stranger's garden. I really wouldn't. Would you? I bet you wouldn't.'

The boy looked at the troll. He had never seen a troll before, but he had surfed the net and so he knew a thousand things about trolls. And this was a troll. It couldn't be anything else: those huge ears attached to a face that wasn't that big. Well, not big enough for the ears anyhow! And that nose. Why, that was a troll nose, if ever there was one.

'You're a troll,' he said touching the troll's head.

'This is my lucky day,' thought the boy. 'This really is my lucky day. I've always wanted to

meet a troll and is this a troll! It is small. Oh, yes, it is a very small troll. But what troll ears, what a troll nose and that hair growing on his head like a piece of lawn that's gone and got itself lost. Boy, is this my lucky day!'

'I know what you are thinking,' said the troll looking at

him with huge round eyes surrounded by wrinkles as if he had been born a hundred and fifty years old. 'I know just what you are thinking, and this might not be your lucky day. Well, it depends on you. It might, it might not.' And the troll laughed. His laughter was so loud that it filled the boy's head till he could almost feel it bursting. He put his hands over his ears and looked down at the troll. He looked and he looked but all he could see was the troll.

'Where is your dog?'

The troll was holding a lead in his hand. It was a long lead and it lay on the grass like a snake. Just beyond it was a small blue cloth rabbit with a cloth carrot in its mouth.

'You can't see my dog,' said the troll smiling as if he were saying something terribly clever. 'You can't see it because it's invisible! But you can see my dog's rabbit just there.' And he pointed.

The boy looked at the rabbit.

'How can I be sure that you have a dog, if it's invisible?'

'Because you can hear it,' replied the troll. 'Just listen.'

The boy could hear that there was something very close to the cloth rabbit, something that was doing a lot of sniffing in the way dogs do when they want to get to know something or someone.

'That's my dog,' said the troll. 'It's a really great sniffer. One of the greatest sniffers in the world. I'm very lucky that it belongs to me. Can you feel him sniffing your feet?'

'Can I feel it!' shouted Henry jumping and laughing. 'That dog has got a tongue that tickles and tickles so I can't stand still.'

'That's why he's called Tickles,' whispered the troll and his voice was so low that Henry had to bend down to hear him. 'He is quite a big dog really. Bigger than me.'

'But you are a very small troll,' said Henry bending down even further to hear what he was saying. 'A really, really small troll.'

'The smallest troll in the world,' said the troll and this time his voice was just a little louder. It was a lovely deep voice, not like any voice Henry knew. Listening to it made him feel that something strange was just about to happen and he couldn't wait to find out what it was. He could feel Tickles sniffing each of his toes very carefully and he could hear him, but all he could see was a troll—a small troll with blue eyes and red hair and a short red tail who was looking straight at him.

'I'm the smallest troll in the world and the cleverest so the garingay will never get me.'

'But the garingay aren't real,' said Henry looking deep into the wrinkled face of the troll and smiling. 'That's just my sister talking. She talks rot and rubbish. She doesn't understand what's real and what isn't. Why, she doesn't believe in trolls!'

'She's not the only one,' said the troll. 'But I don't care. Sometimes it's even more fun when people don't believe in you. Then you can really make them jump. Yesterday I made an old lady jump so high into the air she landed on a wall and couldn't get down. Then I made a policeman jump — and a guy out walking his dog! They all jumped onto the same long brick wall and there they all sat, the three of them, shouting 'troll, troll, troll – beware of the troll.' And everyone who saw them just laughed their heads off while I sat under a bush with my tail in my mouth to stop myself laughing too. But I don't like the garingay.

'I don't like them because they get up to all sorts of tricks and trouble. They keep crocodiles, great big invisible crocodiles and Tickles doesn't like crocodiles and these are so fast because

7

they're on roller skates and some of them even use skateboards which just isn't fair because all Tickle has got are his six legs, and he's no good on skates.'

'Six legs?'

'All invisible dogs have six legs so that they can jump twice as high as ordinary dogs. Look, I'll make him jump up that tree.'

The troll was pointing at a big apple tree that was growing in the middle of the lawn. From a branch high up a swing was hanging. It hung so low it almost touched the ground. Henry's father had put up the swing and he had stood at the top of his tallest ladder to reach. Henry could feel a swish in the air as Tickles jumped up. Then he could hear it barking from high up in the apple tree.

'I'll make him paw you that apple.' The troll pointed at a big red apple almost at the top. 'Paw that apple, Tickles, paw it.'

The apple moved backwards and forwards and fell.

'But I don't like the garingay,' continued the troll. 'And Tickles doesn't like them at all. Do you, Tickles?'

'They don't exist. Lucy just made them up,'

said Henry, not feeling at all sure, but Lucy was always just saying things to frighten him or get him into trouble.

'They do exist,' said the troll. 'There are three kinds: the Big, the Bad and the Ugly – but they're not really very different and they're all of them smelly.'

'Do they eat little boys?' asked Henry.

'Don't be silly, of course not, far too chewy. Lucy just made that up.'

'I knew that. She's always making things up.'

'She may have made up the garingay,' said the troll thoughtfully.

'You said they're real!'

"But that doesn't mean that they haven't been made up. Suddenly something is just there, as real as burnt toast, as smelly as my troll feet and a moment ago it wasn't but then someone made it up, someone with special powers,' explained the troll. 'And whatever it is just goes on and on being. But it takes special powers to do that kind of making up.'

'Do you think Lucy's got special powers?' whispered Henry .

'It's the magic of the wood that's got into her, but she doesn't know it. You could tell, couldn't you, that this wood is magic?' The troll whistled and he could hear Tickles jump down from the tree. He felt a rush of air. 'You can feel the magic, can't you?'

'I can,' said Henry looking at the wood. The wood stood there as if it was an ordinary wood. Just a lot of tall trees innocently minding their own business, but he could hear the wind blowing through it and he thought he could hear and feel its magic, awesome magic of the kind that just goes on and on and doesn't stop for anybody, not even a girl like Lucy.

'The garingay live in the middle of the woods in a small house that's almost impossible to find because of all the magic around,' said the troll bending down and stroking Tickles. Henry wished he could see Tickles, but he could feel the swish, swish of his tail.

'There are lots and lots of garingay and they've got an invisible crocodile each,' continued the troll. 'Sometimes, in the dead of night, when everyone is asleep, they take the crocodiles for walks and let them have fun on skateboards. The garingay are tall and slim and the opposite of trolls in every way. Their noses are small, their feet are tiny, but their legs have scales. They wear

10

shoes, fancy shoes with bells on so that you always know that they are coming. They haven't got tails at all, but their ears are pointy and they're very hairy, furry almost, not like trolls who have only got hair on their heads and just a bit here and there on the rest of their body.'

'They must look weird.'

'You're telling me,' shouted the troll. 'I hate the garingay. I really do.'

'How long have they been around?' asked Henry. The troll didn't answer and it felt as if the wood were looking back at him, as if the trees all had eyes and those eyes were on him. Tickles had stopped sniffing at his feet.

'Have there always been garingay in the wood?'

'No, but they've been here a long time, since before I was born.'

'Then Lucy can't have made them up. '

'Why?'

'Because Lucy only invented them this morning.'

'Oh,' laughed the troll. 'That doesn't prove anything. You see, with magic, things can move backwards and forwards. And the garingay would need magic to exist.' He spread out his hands wide. 'Lots of magic, lots and lots, and once there's lots of magic,' whispered the troll, his eyes growing big, 'well then you just never know where you are. Suddenly everything is different and you remember things that weren't there a minute ago!'

'How scary...'

'Can be terrifying.' The troll looked at Henry and nodded. 'Really terrifying if your thoughts come suddenly out of nowhere, but that is magic and you just have to live with it. You can't fight magic, except with more magic.'

'When did the garingay come to the wood?'

'I'm not sure.'

'Before trolls?'

'There's always been trolls, really far back, but the garingay came when I was little or just before I was born. They came in a painted caravan drawn by a lazy old horse called Cloud. The trolls had never seen anything more amazing than that caravan—it was just a riot of colours, a rainbow of brilliant colours, greens that could knock the senses out of you, reds that seemed to have a life of their own, yellows and oranges burning like fire. And the more you looked, the more you saw: dancing monkeys in proud jungle trees, hippos and crocodiles swimming down rivers, parrots and firebirds sailing through the air and screeching like mad. Old Cloud the horse had no hurry in his kind old bones so the trolls could all let their eyes roam and feast. And they did just that, they let their eyes be caught by that amazing jungle being pulled along, that swinging riot of colours and noise. The garingay were singing and the hippos were bellowing. Everything was making the kind of noise it was just born to make. I've seen the caravan because the garingay take it out from time to time and Cloud—who has grown even older—pulls it along as if the day was never ever going to end. They do it for the Grand Garingay's birthday every year. His birthday is on the longest day of the year so that Cloud can take it really easy and he does just that, stopping now and then to hide his face in the grass and eat away while the trolls just look and look.'

'With those round troll eyes.'

'Our round troll eyes are right on that caravan. It's the greatest magic in the world. It beats everything easily. It beats when witches turn lizards and frogs into bats and throw them up into the air to fly away—they do that whenever they've got something to celebrate and want to

13

do it in style. But I'm talking and talking and Tickles is getting bored. Anyway, there was something I was going to tell you.'

'Something you were going to tell me?' And Henry bent down so that his face was close to the troll's. 'You mean me? You came here to tell me something?'

'I did,' said the troll very seriously. His eyes were on his feet in the way of someone who is really trying to put his thoughts together. His feet were huge compared to the rest of him and the toes were splayed out.

'It's like this,' he said finally. 'They want to steal Lucy. They're fantastic stealers—they can steal anything. Just anything at all. And they do that every year. Every year they steal something so fantastic and weird that you just can't believe it. One year they stole the horns off all the unicorns and hid them so that no one could find them. This year they want to do something even better. They want Lucy because she can do magic. She doesn't know it but she can!'

The troll looked at him thoughtfully. 'Some of the best magic the world has ever seen. The way she can invent creatures—why it's mind blowing. And those garingay, when it comes to stealing, why, they are up for anything, even a human.' He stopped speaking as if a small pocket of silence might help Henry understand how the garingay could steal. 'It's awesome. Just awesome the way they steal.'

Henry looked at the wood and thought of the garingay stealing. He imagined their fingers slipping in out and out with a speed that was nobody's business and didn't belong to this planet. Then he closed his eyes and listened to the wind blowing through the wood.

'Troll fingers are small and fat but the garingay have long fingers that move like lightning. Suddenly what they wanted is gone

15

and all you can hear is the garingay laughing. And there is nothing like the wild laughter of the garingay. It's a bit like the roar of the sea.'

The troll bent down and Henry could see that his hand was stroking the dog.

'Good dog, Tickles, good dog. They once stole Tickles and kept him for weeks and weeks. They only gave him back because he was so useless on a skateboard. Every year they've got a dare—something that's really, really difficult to steal, or utterly impossible. Completely impossible—they'll stop at nothing. Everything is worth trying at least once according to the garingay and they really mean it. That's what it says just above the entrance to their part of the wood: *Everything is worth trying at least once. Just do it!* They've tried the craziest things, like stealing the moon out of the sky or a lion's roar. Things you really can't do, but sometimes really crazy ideas do work; like the time they stole all the horns off all the unicorns or the Grand High Witch's familiar. And now a whisper has gone round the wood that they want to steal Lucy and I thought… Well, I thought that I would take a walk in my garden and …' thoughtfully he stroked Tickles. 'And I was just thinking I might bump into you because you often come here.'

16

'In your garden.'

'Yes, in my garden.'

And Henry thought he knew why it might be his garden.

'They stole it didn't they, the garingay – and gave it to you?'

The troll smiled, a huge smile that went almost all the way across his face. He was looking very pleased with himself.

'You don't mind, do you?' he asked. 'It means that it's a magic garden, a really special garden— so you are lucky because you are a guest and you can have a guest pass.'

The troll opened a small red bag which was hanging round his neck and handed him a shiny silver token with the words Guest Pass Magic Garden First Order – Admit One on it.

'You must take very good care of it,' said the troll very seriously. 'Never give it to anyone suspicious—never ever. Anyone who has a guest pass of the first order can talk to trolls or garingay and any other creature who happens to be in the garden. A guest of the second order can see all the things we can see, like Tickles or invisible crocodiles. A guest of the third order,' and the troll's voice became high with excitement. 'Why, a guest of the third order is just like us. He can join in anything, even with the crocodiles on their skateboards. That hardly ever happens—why first order is rare enough. I'll also give you one other thing, but promise you won't tell anyone.'

Henry nodded.

'I will give you a key,' said the troll. 'A key to the wood. The gate is just over there.' He pointed and suddenly Henry could see a gate, a black metal gate in the fence that hadn't been there before. Henry held out his hand and the troll put a key the size of his thumb on the palm of his hand. The troll was just about to go when Henry asked him his name.

'Haven't got one. I'm just the smallest troll in the world. Any troll that reaches higher than your knees isn't me. Also I've got red hair.'

2

Lucy

'Henry,' shouted his mother. 'Henry.'

'You always need to shout ten times for that boy,' said his father. 'You have only shouted twice so you have another eight times to go.'

'That's because he doesn't listen,' said Henry's sister Lucy.

Lucy was sitting in a chair eating a very large piece of chocolate cake. She had been given the cake because she had been good. Lucy was always good. It was as if goodness just stuck to her. It was there even when Henry knew she wasn't being good at all, or had been really nasty and horrible. Now she was eating chocolate cake because she had done lots of star work for mummy. If you copied some writing very carefully, mummy gave you a star or if you wrote down numbers and added them up, you could get a star. When you had twelve stars, you got a piece of chocolate cake and a present and the whole world stood still and admired you for all that cleverness and your brother Henry seemed to lose his eyes looking at each bite of cake as it disappeared. Slowly. Lucy enjoyed that and she was grumpy because Henry wasn't there.

'He doesn't hear you because he's busy talking to trolls,' she said.

'Talking to trolls, that boy is crazy.'

'Yes, he thinks that the garden is full of magic. I told him that the garingay will get him.'

'The garingay?'

'Oh I just made that up. He'll believe anything.'

'I know twenty-six reasons why trolls don't exist,' said her father firmly. 'And I shall tell that boy all twenty-six reasons, if he's not careful.'

Just then Henry entered the room.

'Been talking to trolls, have you?' asked Lucy, putting a very big piece of cake into her mouth and not waiting for an answer.

'How did you know that?' Henry was standing in the middle of the room and he didn't seem in the least worried. Lucy had never heard him so sure of himself and he wasn't even looking at the cake. He was looking straight out through the window and into the garden.

'It's gone,' he said. 'The troll has gone, disappeared.'

'I know twenty-six reasons,' said his father, a very tall man with a firm mouth, small eyes and short curly hair that clung to his scalp. 'I know twenty-six reasons why trolls don't exist. For one, they're make believe, for two, they're not real, for three, they're much too silly even as an idea, for four, I don't know anyone who's ever seen one, for five...'

'I have,' said Henry quietly. 'I have only ever seen one and he was the smallest troll, the smallest in the whole world, but if there's one then there must be others. A bit like mice—if there's one in the house then there must be others. And you can keep all your reasons, all twenty-six, because I don't care.'

'I have only told you four,' said his father but Henry had already gone.

'He's a very strange boy,' said his mother looking out the window at the wood. Then something happened, something really weird: Henry's mum began to wonder whether trolls just might exist. She didn't know why she was wondering that. It wasn't like her to have those kinds of thoughts, not at all. Then she thought

21

she saw something. The something was not very tall, had a tail and very red hair. It was dancing along through the garden towards the wood. She couldn't see its face but she could hear its laughter. The laughter was very deep, like a kind of rumbling coming out of the ground. It was holding a lead in its hand but there was nothing at the other end of that lead. Nothing at all. She closed her eyes and sighed. So trolls did exist. It was as simple as that.

'You shouldn't have told him about the garingay,' she heard herself saying. 'You really shouldn't. The garingay are dangerous. Much more dangerous than the two of you realise.' And with that she left the room.

'She's gone mad too,' whispered Lucy. 'Completely crazy. I made them up. They don't exist. There is no such thing as garingay.' She finished the last piece of chocolate cake licking her fingers very carefully. 'There is no such thing. She is being very, very silly. I just fished that name out of my brain, just like that. I have no idea why it was there. It's a very silly name, garingay. I did it just to wind him up.'

She looked out of the window and she saw something tall and thin and furry. It didn't look human and it didn't look like a troll. It couldn't, of course, because trolls don't exist. This, on the other hand, did. No doubt about that. It was walking round the garden as if it owned it and didn't care. Didn't care if there might be twenty-six reasons why it didn't exist. It was whistling a tune very happily. It wore big shiny shoes that looked like they had bells on them—anyhow the shoes were making a tingling noise. And then her father said, very calmly, in a very low voice, 'that thing out there – well, does a garingay look something like that?' He pointed. 'I mean that thingy over there.' He sounded as if his eyes were seeing something so amazing that the rest of him had become almost frighteningly calm. 'It does look like one doesn't it?' He kept staring, his mouth open, one hand in the air pointing out through the window.

Lucy looked. The more she looked, the more she knew what she was seeing: a garingay, no doubt about it. A tall thin garingay girl who was dancing round the garden, hopping and skipping and throwing her arms about like nobody's business.

'It's a garingay,' said her father firmly. 'And you shouldn't have made her up.'

'I didn't.'

'But you said you did. Just a minute ago.' Her father looked at his watch. 'You said so at roughly ten to two. It's now eight and half minutes to two and there she is. I say that's amazing. Have you been learning magic?' He was looking at her very carefully in that way he had when he was being what he called really logical, someone who had no time for nonsense. As if he could read her thoughts, he said, 'that's a garingay. I know it in my bones. I've no idea how I recognized her but I knew immediately because she's got all those garingay things about her: she's tall, skinny, hairy, tailless— not like trolls who have tails and sometimes tie them into knots when they're thinking really hard. You know your dad, he's got no time for nonsense, none at all, and no time for beating round the bush and saying things like 'maybe'. Two and two are four and that's a garingay.'

He went closer to the window. 'It's a young one, four or five years old and wild like all garingay.' He was smiling as if he was enjoying examining the garingay and saying things about it. He always had a passion for detail. 'It, or rather she, has got yellow hair but it's a wig because she

is practicing disguise. The garingay are so clever at pretending to be other things and other people. That's what makes them so wonderfully and fiendishly dangerous.' He rubbed his hands. 'But you can defeat them at their own game, if you are very cunning.'

Lucy had never seen her father so excited. He had turned away from the window and was looking at her. 'You'd never catch a garingay doing star work!' He threw the words at her as if he were saying something very different, like 'picking her nose' or 'just sitting there.'

'How do you know all of that?' asked Lucy.

'It's obvious. Just look in front of you, at the wood. That wood makes me see things right.'

It was strange listening to him saying all those weird things in a voice she knew so well. Lucy looked at him with big eyes.

'I don't understand what's wrong with you,' he was saying. 'That was a garingay. Why, your mother said that garingay are dangerous. Perhaps she saw one too. Just look out that window.'

And Lucy did. But she didn't see anything because just at that moment the garingay was behind a large apple tree and garingay are very slim and wiry and the crocodile—garingay hardly ever go anywhere without a crocodile—was invisible. All she saw was a small red ball that the garingay and the crocodile had been playing with.

'You are talking rot,' said Lucy. 'Nothing but rot, rubbish and rhubarb. Garingay don't exist. They can't because I made them up!'

'Are you sure?' asked her father looking confused. 'Are you sure that something doesn't exist just because you made it up? I mean it could, you know. It really could. You should never rule that out.' Lucy's eyes were on her father—she'd never heard him talk like that before. So she didn't see the garingay jump out from behind the tree and do a summersault across the lawn.

'There's one there doing a somersault on the lawn. What are you looking at me like that for? I'm only telling you what I see.'

And then Lucy did look and she saw something and what she saw was quite simply fantastic— completely and utterly fantastic. She didn't see a garingay doing a somersault, but at the end of the garden, from one of the branches of one of the trees overhanging it, the trees of the wood, that wood she called creepy but her brother Henry said was magic—well from one of the branches hung a small creature that had to be a troll because it was hanging by its tail. Yes, by its tail. The rest of what was hanging there (small round face, huge eyebrows, hands waving in the air) was kind of human. Kind of, but very wrinkled without being old in the way people are.

'I can see something,' she said.

'It's a troll, isn't it?' Her father was smiling at her and looking really pleased. 'It really is a troll. A troll swinging by its tail. Wow, doesn't that look fun! I wish I were a troll too.'

Lucy couldn't believe what she was hearing. Her father was wishing he were a troll. Her father! The father who had said he knew twenty-six reasons why trolls didn't exist! And the thing in front of her, swinging from a tree, was a troll. No doubt about it. None at all.

'Isn't it funny,' her father was saying. 'That troll has now jumped down from the tree and is walking along with a lead in its hand.'

'Looks like a dog lead.'

'For an invisible dog.'

Then something happened. Something extraordinary. Everything that had happened was hardly ordinary: a garingay on the lawn, a troll in the tree, but something really extraordinary happened. Something unbelievable.

Lucy went into the kitchen and out through the kitchen door, out into the garden. She stood in the middle of the lawn, hands on her hips and shouted. 'Troll,' she shouted. She shouted again and again but the troll had vanished. All she could see was the lead lying on the lawn.

'If you're not careful,' she said slowly and deliberately. 'If you're not careful, you silly troll, why then the yo yitsoo will get you.' She stamped with one foot and lifted a fist into the air. 'The big bad yo yitsoo who's scared of nothing in the whole world will have you for breakfast.' Thoughtfully, she added, 'he'll have you for breakfast and your guts for garters.' She waved her fist at the wood. 'He'll have you for breakfast because that's the kind of guy he is. On a plate, with a croissant!'

She was about to go back inside when she saw that there was a table in front of her. A small round marble table. On it was a glass of orange juice and a plate with a croissant and a small bit of butter. Next to the table was a huge brown bag with the word Breakfast on it in large red letters. And in the bag, his head and shoulders sticking out, was a troll, all tied up.

'Please,' begged the troll. 'Please, please untie

me before the big bad yo yitsoo comes back and has me for breakfast. I'm only a little troll.'

'He can't do that. He can't eat you.' whispered Lucy.

'Why not?' asked the troll, a small tear rolling downs its cheek. 'Can't you read what it says on the bag?'

'Breakfast. It says breakfast in huge red letters.'

'Well there you are.' The troll sighed. 'The yo yitsoo may be on his way any moment and he'll be hungry. Ever so hungry. He might eat you too. He can never stop eating, that's why he is so fat. Some yo yitsoo have got trunks a bit like elephants but not quite as long. They only their use trunks for small things like croissants. For anything big, they use their long fingers. They've got lizard tails and elephant ears and small eyes just like pigs, and some of them wear glasses. They're a sight, I can tell you and they haven't been around in this wood for ages and ages. For so long that we trolls thought they might have gone somewhere else entirely, or simply disappeared.'

'But I just made them up,' said Lucy.

'Did you?' said the troll surprised. 'That was a horrible thing to do. A really horrible thing to do.'

The troll began to jump around in the paper bag. He was shaking all over. Lucy saw that there was a knife on the table. The rope that had been tied round the troll wasn't very strong but the knife wasn't very sharp so it took her some time to free the troll. And just as she had, her father came out into the garden. He was all dressed for work and looked serious as always. Usually he would give her a kiss and say something like, 'see you later alligator, be a good girl.' That's what he would say when he was going off for work, but he didn't say anything like that at all. It was also funny that he was dressed for work because it was Sunday. In his right hand he was carrying a plate and on it was a large chocolate cake covered in candles.

'I wouldn't touch that croissant,' he said. 'It belongs to the yo yitsoo who will be cross enough when he sees that empty paper bag and finds that his breakfast has run away. You think garingay are bad—well you haven't met a yo yitsoo. To be honest, I wouldn't even go there. They're a funny cross between a lizard and an elephant and I know they only just reach your knees but they're the biggest pain in the neck you can imagine. Worse: they're dangerous. Well, you don't have to listen, if you don't want to, but I can think of twenty-six reasons why I wouldn't have anything to do with a yo yitsoo, anything at all.'

Lucy didn't know what to say. This was her father talking and he was saying that he knew twenty-six reasons why one shouldn't have anything to do with a yo yitsoo. Her father who just didn't like anything that was made up. When she was little he had sometimes read books with strange things in them to her, books about wizards and magic. But you could tell that he didn't like it, that he somehow didn't get it. The strange things had the wrong kind of strangeness for him and when he read out loud you could tell that he was all confused by what he was reading. It wasn't that he disapproved, he just couldn't understand what he was reading and so she and Henry didn't ask him to. Once, she thought he had been hurt. 'I just don't have any imagination,' he had said. 'How can a boy be a wizard? That's silly.' And she had said, yes, daddy, very silly and Henry had insisted that it wasn't silly at all. Just like Henry to pick an argument. But now he was standing there in the middle of the lawn talking loudly about garingay and yo yitsoo as if such creatures had always been around and belonged in the world like everything else.

'I'm on my way,' he was saying, 'I'm on my way to see Grandpa Yo Yitsoo who is terribly old but clever and not like the others. That's why I put on my suit. I think he needs respect. He lives,' he pointed, 'in that wood over there, all by himself. It's his birthday. He's a hundred and one, so I'm bringing him this chocolate cake.'

And he walked very slowly towards the wood and right up to the wooden fence. He knocked on the fence and waited. Then he knocked again. He waited patiently, as if he did this every day. Silently the fence slid open and he disappeared into the wood holding the chocolate cake very carefully so that no branches brushed against it. He walked on ahead as if he knew exactly where he was going and the fence closed behind him.

*

'Well someone has taken my breakfast.' The voice was very deep and growly. Lucy looked round to see where it was coming from. 'I'm talking to you,' continued the voice, which was coming from behind a bush. 'So you better listen. No one, but no one has any business interfering with my breakfast.'

From behind the bush appeared something that was a little taller than she was, about the size of her brother Henry. It had glasses, huge eyes, whiskers, magnificent eyebrows, a determined mouth, some shiny green hair and huge brown ears with yellow hoops in them. It was wearing a small, round red hat. The rest wasn't human at all and it was difficult to know what it was. Dragon seemed the safest bet, that combination of what looked like lizard but wasn't — too big and it was standing up—must be dragon. Lucy looked more carefully. She wasn't afraid and she did wonder why. Yes, the glasses, the ears and those eyebrows—that was human. The rest wasn't but it was fantastic, wonderfully fantastic and it was difficult to be really scared of something that was talking about breakfast.

'Did you,' it was asking. 'Did you steal my breakfast? All that's left is that manky croissant and some horrible jam.'

Suddenly Lucy found it difficult to speak. She could feel her body becoming very cold as if some part of her were covered in ice. There was something about the way in which that creature was moving that she didn't like. It stretched itself, it shook its long neck a little like a snake, and the big scales covering its long tail made her think even more of snake. There was something fierce in the way it surveyed the table and croissant and something about the way it waved its claws—yes they were claws not hands, all nails and bone. And inside the mouth there were too many sharp teeth, definitely too many. It was holding the croissant, ripping it slowly with its mouth.

'You shouldn't,' said that voice, that deep, deep voice. 'You really shouldn't have let that troll go. He was only a weeny troll.'

'Eating trolls,' said Lucy very firmly, as firmly as she could manage. 'Eating trolls is very, very bad. Plain wicked.'

'You should have thought of that.' The voice became nothing but laughter, a wind of laughter that blew through the garden like a storm. 'You should have thought of that,' the voice was saying. 'You really should have thought of that before you made me up!'

'Made you up?'

'I'm a yo yitsoo,' whispered the creature. 'I'm a yo yitsoo and I'm out to get trolls. I would have their guts for garters, except I don't know what that means. Do you?' It sounded a little upset. 'I want to do everything right, you know. I haven't been around that long, not long enough to know everything.'

The yo yitsoo was looking at her. It had huge, very round eyes, which lurked behind a pair of dark green glasses. It was wearing a large pink shell round its neck and it noticed that she was looking at it. 'Do you like my shell? I would give it to you, except it's magic, a very beautiful magic.'

'What does it do?'

'If I rub it, I disappear. Then if I whistle through this hole here,' the yo yitsoo pointed to where the shell was attached to a dark piece of string. 'Why, if I whistle through here, then I reappear where I was before. It's ever so useful but I don't use it very often. Would you?'

'I don't know,' said Lucy. 'I wish I had something like that. Then I could really tease Henry.' She was thinking of all the many ways she could tease Henry when the yo yitsoo began to come closer. It had a strange walk as if the garden were the deck of a ship, a rolling walk and it waved its hands with their claw-like fingers as it went along.

'I think you'll be needing Henry,' it said. It put one hand on her shoulder and in order to do that it had to reach up. 'You'll be needing Henry because the garingay are out to get you. Today is their special day and they only do one special thing on their special day, decided long before the day itself, something that can't be changed. This year they want to get you. It's what they want most in the whole world, so they're very likely to do it. They've let it be known, you see, known all over the wood. *We are going to get Lucy and no one is going to stop us.'*

'Why me?'

'Because you don't believe in magic, because you don't believe in trolls or garingay or yo yitsoo.'

And then something very strange happened. Very strange and Lucy couldn't explain it, couldn't explain it all. She was standing there with the wood in front of her, staring at a strange creature that looked like a dragon with human eyes and big human eyebrows but she found herself saying. 'Of course I don't believe in garingay, or trolls or yo yitsoo. Why they don't exist. Not at all. I can think of twenty-six reasons...'

'There you are,' said the yo yitsoo waving its tail. 'There you are. No wonder the garingay just want to steal you. Well I think you'll be sorry...' And the yo yitsoo turned round and began to walk towards the wood.

Why had she said that? She knew that they were all real, dangerously real. But the wood made you do strange things. Sometimes looking at it, you said things you didn't mean at all.

'I must speak to Henry,' thought Lucy. Henry understood the wood. Henry knew that trolls were real.

3

Fiendish

'Henry,' shouted Lucy. 'Henry!'

Where had that boy gone now that she needed him? He was nowhere in his room. The place was a mess, a total catastrophe of what not; the remains of a feast among the bedclothes; crisps, an empty bottle of coca cola, a bounty bar wrapper. On the floor clothes—underwear, socks and toys.

'Henry,' shouted Lucy. 'Henry!'

He couldn't be far. The room felt of Henry. It even smelled of Henry.

'Henry!'

'Lucy!'

There he was, right outside the window. His face looked full of secrets he wanted to share. There was that wait-till-I-tell you smile. And Lucy remembered that sometimes, just sometimes, there was no one, but no one, she wanted to be with more than Henry, that brother Henry. She went up to the open window on tiptoe, quietly. She hadn't noticed that it was open, and now, looking out into the garden, she thought she could feel that there was something out there, something creepy.

'Henry,' she whispered.

She didn't want any of them to hear her, the trolls, the garingay, the yo yitsoo or anything else that might be lurking outside. Any other creatures that might be there living and breathing in that wood, or in the garden, walking their invisible dogs or crocodiles.

'Henry,' whispered Lucy.

'Shhh. We must beware of the garingay.'

'And the yo yitsoo.'

'Yo yitsoo? What's that? I haven't heard of that.'

'It's kind of like a dragon—the back bit. The back bit is all scales and dragon, but small and the front bit has a face that's kind of human with eyebrows and glasses. It'll eat a troll for breakfast, if it can lay hands on one.'

'And if it can't?'

'Croissant, butter and jam.'

'Sounds awesome.'

'It is awesome. And...' she paused feeling she

41

was going to say something big and dangerous that Henry had to know. 'And… and I made it up! I made up the yo yitsoo. I know I did. I know I did!'

'How did you do that?'

'I sort of imagined it and then I said it, said its name. I said "yo yitsoo" really loudly and waited. I was really angry with this little troll who had vanished into the wood and that made me angry. So I shouted, "yo yitsoo!"'

'Did he have red hair?'

'A load of red hair. Like a carpet on his head, so thick and bright red like he was on fire. He was in the garden. Really tiny he was.'

'The smallest troll in the world.'

'You know him?'

'Kind of. What did you shout?'

'If you're not careful, silly troll, then the yo yitsoo will get you and have you for breakfast and your guts for garters.'

'Guts for garters! How horrible.' Henry's eyes had grown bigger and rounder. 'Guts for garters!' He whispered and she could hear him catch his breath.

'Then a yo yitsoo appeared and there was this table with a plate and croissant and by the table was a brown bag, a big brown paper bag. On it was written Breakfast in funny letters as if someone was just learning how to write.'

'And inside that brown paper bag was the smallest troll in the world,' said her brother. 'The smallest troll in the world waiting to be eaten for breakfast just because you made up a yo yitsoo. That was horrible, really horrible. And awesome.' He closed his eyes and sighed.

'It's the wood,' said his sister—his sister who not long ago knew nothing about anything. 'It's the wood,' she was saying. 'That wood gives me magic. It gives me magic, whether I want it or not.'

Henry nodded. You couldn't do anything about that wood. You couldn't control it. It was there whether you wanted it or not. It was full of magic, whether you wanted it or not, and it contained strange creatures. Some were good, that troll was a good troll, but some were bad and awesome in their badness and you couldn't read their thoughts or know what they wanted to do, but you could be certain of one thing: some of them wanted to do things so badly that no one could stop them. No one in the whole world.

"There is something I must tell you,' whispered Henry. 'It's about the garingay. '

'I know,' said Lucy. 'I know.'

'They're out to get you.'

Lucy nodded.

'We need a plan,' said Henry. 'A really fine plan.'

Lucy looked at Henry and she knew that he didn't have a plan. His eyes were big and empty and his fingers were playing with a crisp packet. He was sitting next to her on the bed.

Suddenly she saw something in the garden. The something was a troll. The smallest troll in the world just walking around with a lead and whistling. The troll waved at her. She waved back and the troll came closer. Then he jumped through the open window into Henry's room and sat down on the bed. He seemed very comfortable. The bedroom was full of the kind of darkness you find when the curtains are drawn but it's day outside, a speckled darkness full of shadows and shafts of light.

'The meeting has started,' said the troll.

They both looked at him.

'The meeting has started,' repeated the troll. 'A meeting to make a plan.'

He was very serious and they became serious too. Lucy had never seen Henry so serious. He looked as if he really understood, too. As soon as the troll had jumped through the window, he had become a different Henry. She felt as if she knew this Henry and trusted him. They were sitting on his bed right next to each other. And in front of them was a troll.

'The yo yitsoo,' the troll was saying waving his right arm in the air. 'The yo yitsoo must be banished from the wood, and the garingay must be defeated but first...' the troll paused and seemed to retreat into his own thoughts.

'First?' asked Henry.

'First,' repeated the troll thoughtfully and sighed. 'First we must talk about you, Lucy, and the wood. That wood does things to all of us but what it does to you is really awesome.'

They both nodded.

'I don't understand what has been happening to me,' she whispered feeling afraid of what she was saying. 'When I make up something it becomes real. I made up the garingay and I made up the yo yitsoo.'

'Did you make up me?' asked the troll.

'I don't think so, but I'm not sure. I can't remember.' She looked at him very closely.

'Trolls can't be made up,' said Henry. 'There

have been trolls as far back as anyone knows and further back than that. Much further. There have been trolls,' he paused thoughtfully, 'before humans, but early humans and trolls, they knew how to get on. There are stories of them hunting woolly mammoths together and sitting round fires roasting huge hunks of meat and telling jokes. But there were trolls before that. Humans only appeared around the end of that time, woolly mammoth time, but trolls were there at the beginning and I've heard that in those days they used to get on well living together in caves. At night, the trolls would snuggle up to the woolly mammoths and lie snoring between their long curved tusks. During the day, they would tramp about on that vast thing called tundra and the woolly mammoths would listen to all the stories the trolls had to tell because trolls are always doing that, telling stories. So Lucy can't have made you up, no way.'

'You're sure?' asked the troll. 'Quite sure? I don't want to be made up. That's horrible. The yo yitsoo don't seem to mind, but I suppose they haven't got any choice.'

'No choice at all,' whispered Lucy and a shiver went down her spine. She put her hand over her mouth. She had to stop herself from saying a strange sound that would become a name, the name of some creature with its own will and things it liked to do.

'Don't worry,' said the troll. 'You're not looking at the wood. You have to look at the wood to do magic.'

'Zing Zang,' said Lucy. 'Fiendish Zing Zang, as big as cats, with eyes that glow and claws like razors.'

There was an awesome silence in the room but nothing happened. Nothing at all. She jumped off the bed and looked out the window.

'Fiendish...'

The troll had his hand round her mouth. She felt herself falling. Henry's voice, loud, frightened, 'why did you do that?'

She didn't reply. She didn't know what to say. I did it because it felt fun, because it's dangerous. She couldn't say that.

'Get up,' said the troll.

'Don't ever do that again,' said Henry.

'Course not,' she heard herself saying wondering how she could be saying that. It was just so not true, even if a bit of her—perhaps most of her—wanted it to be true. It was too tempting. Now that she knew what would happen, she couldn't wait to see it happening. To see some creature suddenly appear from nowhere—not quite from nowhere, from her head, what a curious head—and stand there in front of her with the looks she had given him.

'Look,' Henry was shouting and pointing out into the garden. 'Just look!'

'What is it?' she asked shrugging her shoulders to show she didn't care.

'I don't know,' said Henry very slowly. 'It is very small and jumpy like a monkey. Small and fury,' he added thoughtfully. 'But when it looks at you it looks, well, kind of fiendish. Something about it is kind of fiendish. The eyes, perhaps. Or the whole thing—whatever it is. Look the way it is crouching behind that bush as if it were trying out how to lurk.'

'Well,' said Lucy. 'That's probably what it's doing. I mean, it hasn't been around for long. It's still trying things out. And it's pretty good at it. It's really lurking. Doing some good lurking.' She was enjoying talking and she discovered she had a liking for this creature, this creature she had made.

'I don't think that you can stop now. Not now.' She could feel the troll's hairy hand touching hers. 'I think you should finish him.'

'Finish him?'

'He isn't finished.'

'He's fiendish,' explained her brother. 'You should make him fiendish at something.'

'Make him a fiendishly good spy who likes trolls.'

'And can make himself invisible,' whispered Lucy looking at the bush outside. 'Can make himself invisible when he is in real danger, or when he feels like it because it's just the thing to do. Just the perfect thing to do.' She was breathing heavily but air had never felt so light. 'He's looks like a monkey, but with a touch of fiendish because he's fiendishly clever and fiendishly quick and knows more about how to spy than all the world put together. But he likes trolls. Small trolls with red hair and he hates garingay and yo yitsoo because that's the way he's made and he can't do anything about it even if he tried…'

Something was standing next to her. It didn't quite reach her shoulders. A small face with huge round eyes was looking up at her. He had jumped in through the open window.

He looked at her and pulled a face. Then he laughed. Next he hurled himself onto the bed and wrapped himself in a bit of the duvet that was hanging over the end.

'The meeting,' her brother was saying. 'The meeting has started.'

*

For a few minutes they just sat looking at each other and getting used to each other's presence. The troll seemed calm compared to the new creature who was continually moving about. First he rolled himself up in as much duvet as he could without making Henry and Lucy fall off the bed, then he unrolled himself, jumped off the bed and went over to the bookshelf. He took down a couple of books, examined them as if he had never seen anything like that before and had no idea what they might be for. He took a big bite out of one, spat it out and returned to the bed. He had huge feet and a nice way of bouncing on them.

'What's your name?' asked Henry.

'What a silly, silly question,' laughed the creature, looking at his toes with their shiny blue nails almost lost among all that fur. 'That's just so silly. My name is Fiendish.'

Henry and Lucy looked at him and nodded. Of course that was his name. He couldn't have any other. He was Fiendish. And the name suited him in spite of the childish way he had of bouncing up and down and of tearing things apart or trying to eat them. He was fiendish, you could tell that.

'The plan,' he was saying, 'is simple. The garingay want to get Lucy. It's their next BIG THING. They've stolen the horns of all the unicorns and they once hid the moon for a week, but they've never stolen a human and they want Lucy.' He paused, planted his small hairy arms with their long hairy fingers on his knees and laughed. Lucy, Henry and the troll were silent. They were looking at him and listening to his laughter while they waited for him to continue. They had never sat so still.

'But we're not scared,' continued Fiendish and

winked. 'We won't even hide. We'll go straight into the enemies' camp, into the wood. Yes, the wood is waiting. What fun,' he shouted jumping up and hitting the lamp hanging down from the ceiling so that it swung round and round. 'What fun!'

'And then?' asked the troll.

'You'll just have to trust me,' said Fiendish.

'I don't like that,' said the troll. 'Trolls don't trust anyone. That's the way we are.'

'I know,' said Fiendish. 'I know, but trolls will have to change. You will all have to change. You won't be the same again. No one is once they have met me!'

Again he laughed. What laughter! Henry looked at Lucy and Lucy looked at Henry. They knew just what the other was thinking: this is going to be such fun. They couldn't really believe what they were thinking because it was also going to be dangerous and scary. Henry wondered whether being with Fiendish wasn't a bit like having the wood in your bedroom. Just like the wood, he did things to your brain. Lucy was pinching him in a way that meant that she felt just like he did. He had never been so close to his sister—that sister! The sister who used to do star work! She had a look in her eye that was very difficult to imagine in the eye of someone who did star work. But then, everyone was changing. His father—the father who knew twenty-six reasons why trolls didn't exist—why that father had wandered into the wood as if he belonged there, with a cake in his hand, a chocolate cake for Grandpa Yo Yitsoo who was, he said, one hundred and one. It was unbelievable. And there in front of them was a troll and something called Fiendish.

'What do the garingay want with me?' asked Lucy.

'They want your magic. They're mad about magic. They want to steal it.'

'You can't steal magic,' said Lucy in a voice Henry recognized. It was the voice that had said that trolls don't exist. But then her eyes met those of Fiendish and he could feel that she was a different person now. The way she looked at Fiendish, as if they were on the same side, was a new way of looking, a good way of looking. One you could trust.

'You can steal anything,' said Fiendish. 'Any-thing in the world, and the garingay know that. They're the most awesome stealers you could ever imagine.'

Lucy had never come across a really good stealer, not anyone who was in the least awesome, so she listened in silence.

'They'll steal things with such speed and lightness that you don't even notice that it's gone. You'll swear that they didn't even touch you and yet it's gone, the mobile, the sandwich, the bubble gum, that bit of chocolate you've been saving. Whatever they wanted, whatever they decided to steal, has vanished. If they steal you, it will take you some time to notice. At first, you'll just think that you have got lost. That's how clever they are. You could say they are fiendishly clever, except that is going too far—much too far. There is only one Fiendish and that's me.'

The creature jumped onto the bed and started throwing the pillows into the air.

'I'm the only Fiendish,' sang the creature, jumping about. 'The only Fiendish in the world...'

The door opened and a head appeared around it. The head was looking at them thoughtfully but not saying anything. The head belonged to their father. They both looked down at the floor wondering what he would say. What he would say when he saw something that looked a bit like a monkey, a bit like a cat, and a bit, thought Henry, just a tiny bit like a kangaroo? It was that way it had of resting on its long flat feet. Oh, he had never seen anything like it and someone who could think of twenty-six reasons why trolls don't exist would think of a least a hundred why…

'I have heard all about Fiendish,' their father was saying. 'I have heard all about Fiendish from Grandpa Yo Yitsoo—he loved his chocolate cake by the way and well, who wouldn't? Most of us can think of at least ten reasons why chocolate cake is good but I won't mention any because we have important business to discuss. Well, Grandpa Yo Yitsoo thinks it was very clever of you,' he was looking at Lucy, 'really clever of you to invent Fiendish. 'He's just what they need,' he said. 'Just what they need to deal with the garin-gay.' And I agree. Though I wouldn't go any-where without a troll. I can think of twenty-six reasons why people always need trolls—the trollier the better that is reason number one. Life is better when it's trollier, reason number two. It trolls along better, reason number three. You can't trust a human that doesn't believe in trolls—that's reason number four. So if you've got one, others have to believe in them.' He was looking at them very carefully in that way he had when he wanted to make sure that you were listening. Then, suddenly, he slammed the door. They could hear his heavy footsteps down the hall, and the front door being opened and closed. Then silence.

'He's right,' said the troll.

'Dead right,' said Fiendish. 'And we must stick together. And now for the first step of our fiendish plan. There's a meeting tonight of the garingay. The Chief Garingay has called it. We must know what happens.' He was looking at the troll. 'A small job for your invisible dog. A small job for Tickles…'

4

Tickles

Tickles was lying on the floor underneath the table. He was lying there so that no one would step on him. If you are invisible, you have to make sure that no one falls over you. It's quite difficult being invisible, but Tickles was used to it because he had been invisible all his life. Being invisible can be lonely but Tickles didn't mind because he lived with trolls and trolls have a wonderful knack with invisible creatures. They know how to make them feel needed and appreciated which isn't a straightforward thing at all. Lots of people wouldn't know what to do with an invisible dog. Tickles sniffed the floor carefully: there was a nice little chocolate biscuit not far from his mouth but he thought he had better not try to eat it because then someone might hear him chewing. Some magical creatures have fantastic ears.

The garingay were sitting round the table. He could hear the claws of the oldest garingay drumming the table impatiently. He was in charge and he seemed really grumpy.

Tickles let his tongue feel its way along the floor towards the biscuit hopefully but then he changed his mind and lay very still.

'We have decided to take her.' The Chief Garingay was saying. 'And that's what we are going to do.' His hand stopped drumming. 'We don't change our minds. I'm speaking for all of us, not just myself.'

'Of course you are. Stealing her will be just glorious.' The voice was low and perhaps evil. The way it said 'glorious'. His tongue went out again. This time it returned with the biscuit. Slowly he let it crumble and melt in his mouth while he listened.

'We want her,' said another voice.

'That way she has of not believing in anything!'

'We'll teach her!'

Tickles wondered how many garingay were sitting round the table. Each voice had belonged to someone different. There was the feel of many presences, too many.

'Of course we'll teach her,' the Chief Garingay

was saying. 'Someone like that has to be taught a lesson. I don't mind that she doesn't believe in trolls—but not to believe in garingay!'

Laughter rippled round the room.

'They're evil,' thought Tickles. 'Just plain evil but I can deal with that. I'm a clever dog. And I've come across evil before. It's been around for a long time. Even longer than garingay or trolls. It was there back in the early days of woolly mammoth, before they had made friends with trolls and were just wandering around thinking that the world was an easy place and you could just be yourself. Then they discovered evil lurking in some small canny creatures living in those endless woods among all that snow and icicles.'

'She'll regret it,' continued the Chief Garingay. 'And by that I mean really regret it. How can she not believe in us when she made us up?'

'She didn't. She didn't! No one made us up!' The voices sounded shrill, desperate and very young. 'Please, say she didn't!'

'I'm sorry to have to tell you,' said the Chief Garingay firmly. 'But there's no doubt about it, we're made up. It's a terrible thing to have to admit, a really humongously bad thing — and I only do it because there's no way around it. But it's just the way it is: we're made up. But who cares? Most of the time we don't give it a thought. How many of you,' the claws hammered the table. 'How many of you wake up in the morning saying sadly, 'I'm made up'. Not one of you! It just doesn't happen.'

The claws stopped, one of his feet kicked out under the table. Tickles could feel it just grazing his tail.

'There is something under this table,' muttered the Chief Garingay in a horrible aside. 'There is definitely something under this table,' he shouted angrily.

Chairs were pushed back, faces were looking at him but of course they didn't see anything. Nothing at all.

'I can't see anything.'

'Nor can I.'

'Nothing at all.'

A door opened.

'What are you all doing there, on your hands and knees and bottoms in the air?' Someone had just entered the room.

'Looking for something under the table.'

'Grandpa Sam thought there was something under the table,' said one of the smaller garingay who only had so much respect for the Chief Garingay.

'He's always imagining things,' said another casually.

And another, 'there's is nothing at all under this table.'

There was the sound of getting up, of chairs being pulled forwards. Tickles opened his eyes. The feet were back in place.

'I don't imagine things,' said the Chief Garingay calmly. 'I never do. But I know when I feel something. There is something under the table and it better watch out. When I lay my hands on it, it will regret it.'

His legs kicked the air as if searching for something. Slowly Tickles moved away but he had to be careful. There were feet everywhere and he couldn't trust them not to move.

'Why have you come?' asked the Chief Garingay.

'I just wanted to tell you something,' said a growly voice. A couple of garingay coughed. The Chief Garingay kicked and grazed one of Tickles' paws.

'The thing I wanted to tell you is that she has done it again.'

'Done what and who is she?'

'You know who I mean. That girl Lucy. She

has invented something. She has invented Fiend-ish.'

'That… that's terribly, fantastic, gremlicious and rapscallious,' said the Chief Garingay thoughtfully. 'But I'm not at all surprised. That girl has got gumption and ants in her pants. That's why we want to steal her. That's why we must steal her. And then we will take away her magic and I'll put it in my pocket where it belongs, where all magic belongs. And then I'll take that little troll with the red hair, and hip hop, I'll tie him up and you can have him for breakfast together with that silly-Billy invisible dog that he goes around talking to, that Tickles.'

'How can I eat something that is invisible? Bet it won't taste of anything.'

'Bet it will, bet you have never tried. Bet it will taste of mushrooms and garlic and be utterly scrumdiddly.'

'Bet you have forgotten that she has invented Fiendish.'

'Do I forget? I am the Chief Garingay! I never forget, but sometimes…' he sounded as if he was tasting the words. 'Sometimes I just let my mind stray elsewhere, butterfly about. So she has invented Fiendish. Well, he was kind of waiting for that. Someone had to invent him. Didn't we all kind of want to? But she got there first because she's got the magic and she doesn't even know it! It's disgusting, that's what it is. Disgusting and evil.' His claws slid across the table. 'Very evil, but I'm going to put that right. Very right, because I'm evil too.'

'Not as evil as Grandpa Yo Yitsoo.'

'Shut up. Evil? He doesn't know the meaning of that word. He's been sitting all day eating chocolate cake with her dad, the guy with the twenty-six reasons for this and that— why trolls don't exist, why you should eat your breakfast or not pick your nose.'

'Don't wind me up,' said the creature who had just entered. Tickles found a gap between the legs and feet and stuck his head out from under the table. It had a long tail and it was very scaly, big green shiny scales. So he must be a yo yitsoo, one of those terrible creatures that ate trolls for breakfast and wanted their guts for garters. He shivered and closed his eyes.

'Don't wind me up,' repeated the creature who must be a yo yitsoo. 'Don't make me angry. We must stick together – all of us, garingay and yo yitsoo. We really must.'

'Why?' asked one of the garingay and they all laughed that wicked garingay laughter that sounded like gargling with saw dust.

'Because,' said the yo yitsoo, 'because we have been invented.'

'And?' asked a voice.

'It's very simple, if you can remember you can forget.' He paused as if he was going to say something very important. 'Everything has its opposite.'

'So if you can be invented...'

'Then you can be un-invented or kind of wiped out.'

Silence.

'And we wouldn't want that to happen, would we?'

'Does she know how to do it?'

'Who?'

'Lucy!'

'She doesn't know what she can do! She is so human. They never know what they can or can't do, their thoughts just jump about like grasshoppers this way and that,' continued the yo yitsoo darkly. 'But that is the problem. Just when you think that you have got them, why then they slip through your fingers and do something, close,' he whispered his eyes growing huge. 'Ever so close to impossible. Why she might be here, might be here lurking under the table invisible!'

'What!' shouted a dozen garingay hammering the table till it shook and Tickles made himself into a six legged ball of fur in a bit of a space that seemed to be getting smaller and smaller.

'I only said she might be here.'

The table stopped moving but Tickles hardly dared to breathe.

'I only said might.' The yo yitsoo walked up to where the Chief Garingay was sitting. Tickles could see his big claw feet and his dragon tail.

'Of course it might be Tickles.'

'Tickles?'

'Tickles— that dog the little troll is always taking for walks.'

'I had forgotten about him,' muttered the Chief Garingay and sighed. Tickles tried not to breathe.

'I wouldn't worry about him,' said the yo yitsoo firmly and Tickles allowed himself to open one eye and look at his tail. 'We must just concentrate on real danger. We must not, I repeat, we must NOT let ourselves be uninvented.' His tail swished back and forth emphasizing the seriousness of what he was saying. 'Uninvention must be a no go area, a place you don't even think about, even if it lives and breathes in your worst dreams. She must,' he drew a deep breath. He sounded desperate. 'She must NEVER do that. Not EVER. Somehow we must stop her.'

'Why,' asked a garingay, it sounded like a young garingay, his voice was so squeaky. 'Why should she want to?'

'Why should she want to!' Boomed the yo yitsoo hammering the table. 'Why that is obvious, it's as much fun to uninvent as it is to invent—only she hasn't tried it. Not yet. She hasn't tried looking at that wood and ...'

'Be quiet,' hissed the Chief Garingay loudly. 'Don't say another word! I think there's something under the table.'

And then they all looked—more eyes than he could count were looking at Tickles.

'He's there,' said the Chief Garingay. 'Only he is fiendishly invisible.'

He stuck his head under the table and was feeling his way creeping along on all fours. He had almost reached Tickles.

'Don't say that word!' shouted the yo yitsoo as if his pants were on fire. 'Just don't say that word!'

Slowly the Chief Garingay got up from his knees and blew his nose. There was a long squeaky sound as if he had finally dislodged some obstacle in a tired trumpet. Then a muffled laughter. That must the young garingay. The feet retreated.

'What word, stupid? What word, idiot? What bloody word?' shouted the Chief Garingay angrily thumping the table. 'Why do you have to fill your talk with things I don't understand? And I'm not an idiot you know, not at all, at all. Not even the tiniest, weeniest bit! You, you think you know everything just because you are a yo yitsoo. There have been creatures who think like that since the beginning of time and even further back than that— before there were human beings running around on two legs— and what hap-

67

pened to them, all those clever creatures? They all went the way of the dinosaurs. All that cleverness got them nowhere. Bam, bam, out! Even the Tyrannosaurus Rex has had it. And he thought he knew everything just because he was good at squishing and squashing things, better than anyone before or since and boy, did that give him big ideas. Still, he was around much longer than any yo yitsoo. So what word mustn't I say? Speak up, I'm all ears.' He cupped one hand round a hairy ear the size of a tray.

'Fiendish — you mustn't breathe that word — it gives me the creeps,' whispered the yo yitsoo humbly. 'Please...'

'Of course it gives you the creeps,' said the Chief Garingay calmly. 'We are all afraid of Fiendish. He's brainy, pure brains. Why did she have to invent him? We would be doing alright without him. But there he is, and on their side too! But he too can be uninvented,' said the garingay thoughtfully flicking a piece of cake across the table. There was a huge plate in front of him covered in cup cakes, but no one had touched it. Now they all reached out.

'Hands off!' shouted the Chief Garingay. 'Hands off my cakes. They're special.'

'How special?' asked the yo yitsoo.

'Not telling!' And the Chief Garingay laughed. He laughed and laughed and his laughter was like nothing Tickles had ever heard before. It was very SCARY. It boomed and echoed. It hurt his ears.

'Now,' continued the voice of the garingay in a great roar. 'Now you must all promise to help me steal Lucy. We shall sneak in at the dead of night and catch her unawares.'

'What does that mean?' asked the yo yitsoo. 'And who's trying to be clever? Unawares, my bottom, by all the bogeys in my nose, what does that mean?'

'It means before she's had time to say fiendish, before she even knows it, she's gone, inside a sack and right here in front of me, in this very room, that's what it means.' He drummed his nails on the table. No one spoke. Tickles could hear the Chief Garingay push back his chair. He stood up. The yo yitsoo was standing next to him. Tickles could see his long scaly legs at the end of the table and his big feet with their enormous toes and long, dark nails. He wanted to sink his teeth into one of those fat toes. He closed his eyes. That wouldn't be clever. Thoughtfully, he licked one of his paws.

'Tomorrow. We must all be ready for tomorrow. First there's the party...'

'Party?' interrupted the yo yitsoo. 'No one told us about a party.'

'Perhaps no one wanted to invite you,' said a small voice coming from the head of the table. 'We don't want any horrible yo yitsoo at our party.'

There was lots of giggling and clapping and then a loud thump.

'Don't be silly,' said the Chief Garingay banging the table. 'Everyone is welcome, but dressed up. It's a pirate party. No one is allowed in unless they've got something pirate about them. The whole place is going to look like a ship with rigging, sails and what not. And they've even made a lookout which is going to hang from the mast and I'm going to sit in it, the biggest pirate of all. The biggest pirate the world has ever known. It's my birthday and I want a pirate party for my birthday because I've always wanted to sail the seven seas. There's adventure in my bones and I'm brave as a lion, I can tell you, and you can take my word for it because I'm the biggest garingay that ever was.'

'And the biggest idiot too,' thought Tickles.

'Pirate! You're just somebody Lucy has invented, and what can be invented can be uninvented…'

He could hear them leaving. The room became dark.

Tickles came out from under the table. His eyes were looking round at everything. He saw very well in the dark because invisible dogs are particularly good at seeing in the dark and moving in the dark. He jumped up on the table and with a quick sweep of one paw all the cup cakes disappeared into a little sack he was carrying. He wondered why they were special. He wondered when the garingay would try to steal Lucy. He knew it would be soon. He thought about the little troll and swore that no yo yitsoo would ever have him for breakfast or his guts for garters. Not ever.

He slung the sack over his back and stood on two legs to open the door. Very slowly. And no one heard him. No one at all.

5

The cupcakes

Lucy and Henry kept looking towards the window hoping that Tickles would soon be back. They had left the window slightly open. It was cold outside, and it was getting very cold inside. He seemed to have been away for ages. What were those garingay up to? He and Lucy had done a lot of talking but neither Fiendish nor the troll had said a word.

They were busy making a castle of cards and their talent was awesome. The way they could balance cards on their noses was amazing. But it didn't make Henry forget about the garingay. Right now Fiendish was on the floor adding the thirteenth floor to the castle. The cards made patterns that seemed to ignore gravity but neither of them ever looked surprised. They just kept taking cards out of their sleeves and pockets as if they could just go on doing that forever. The cards looked really weird. There were kings, queens and jacks holding strange creatures and objects and some of them had a way of looking at you that they both found scary. Only the Queen of Hearts smiled but she wasn't looking at them. She was smiling at a small dragon at her feet blowing smoke that curled all around her head. The castle had windows and a drawbridge and on the very top, the thirteenth floor, there was a dragon. Fiendish was just finishing his tail. With his thumbs he held the cards steady. He had huge hands and he had a way of holding the cards that made Henry feel that he was in control. Perhaps the garingay couldn't get them. Perhaps. Fiendish showed them his last two cards: two jokers. One had green hair, the other bright red. Their hair stood out from their heads like the rays of the sun. They reached out and shook hands with each other and when Henry and Lucy looked surprised they winked. Then they put their hands behind their backs and stood very still and closed their eyes.

Just then something came through the window. A bag, followed by a whirl of air blowing the castle over and scattering the cards all over the room. Tickles! There was a sound of feet and the smell of wet dog. A big green bag made of some thick material lay on the floor and the invisible Tickles was pushing it towards the little troll. Henry and Lucy's eyes were on the bag. It was moving as if it contained something alive. Without thinking, Henry put his arm round Lucy and she didn't push him away. The troll picked up the bag with two hairy fingers.

'What's in here?' he whispered sniffing it while scratching one ear thoughtfully. The bag was almost the size of him. He really was small and wonderfully ugly. His head was round and wrinkled liked a baked apple. His mouth was huge and he had eyebrows that reminded Henry of foxtails. He was concentrating terribly on that bag, feeling it and sniffing it. You could tell that he wasn't the sort to give up easily. Carefully, he extracted something from the bag and held it up to his eyes. It didn't look like anything much, just a cake. But the troll was fascinated.

'Garingay cup cakes,' came a voice somewhere close to the troll's hairy feet with their huge hairy toes. 'Garingay cup cakes. They smell of honey, ginger and elephant dung. I didn't know whether they might be useful or really bad. I took a chance because I couldn't stop myself from picking up that bag. It just had pick me up written all over it.'

'And it's got eat me written all over!'

'And turn into something and I-wish-I-hadn't,' shouted Henry grabbing the cup cake from the troll's hairy fingers that would not let go. The troll was really quite fat. He hadn't noticed that before. The troll had been perfect—just right. Yes, small but in all ways what you might expect of a troll. Henry realized that he had no idea what to expect of a troll. Trolls were an unknown country. This troll said he was the cleverest troll in the world but he could be tricked; tricked by a cup cake made (possibly) of lemon, ginger, elephant dung and very likely something else. His mouth had become an angry trumpet that made his big nose seem smaller and his face squashed. Those thick eyebrows really did look like foxtails and now they were slanting like arrows and pointing up at his thick, wild hair. In one hand he held the cake, while with the other he drew a shape in the air, a dog's back. Some thought was bothering him but slowly his face relaxed and he put the cake down and sighed.

"There's something in those cakes. They are too tempting. Boy, does that wicked Grandma

Yo Yitsoo know how to make cakes. She's evil.'

All the while, Lucy's eyes had been on the cake. Suddenly she looked round and grabbed it like a thief. She put both hands around it as if it were treasure.

'You don't like cup cakes,' said Henry. 'You are always saying they are dead boring unless they're chocolate. And this one is made of ginger and elephant dung!'

'I don't care. It's mine!'

She was holding it so tight that an ordinary cupcake would have crumbled. Her fingers were all sweaty and between them a slow thick brown liquid was beginning to trickle. Henry felt his eyes becoming mesmerized. Lucy was holding that cake as if everything else had slipped her thoughts. He had never seen her so absorbed. It was scary.

She put it to her nose. Henry knew that he ought to stop her. She could do magic but she didn't always see where it was. Lucy didn't really understand magic, she just used it. He knew that he should grab the cake. She kept sniffing it slowly and thoughtfully. He could still stop her. Fiendish was collecting up the cards. They must be special cards because he was taking great care with them. Tickles was breathing very evenly. He must have fallen asleep. The troll was looking straight at Lucy and Henry could see that a thought was lurking in his head. Then he winked at Henry and Henry knew that they were both waiting for something to happen.

'Maybe,' said the troll.

'Maybe what?' Lucy was lifting the cake above her head as if she had won it and it was the most important prize in the world. She closed her eyes and put the cake to her lips, kissing it. Then she put it to her nose and breathed deeply.

The troll shrugged his shoulders as if to say that he couldn't help. One of the jokers on the floor caught Henry's eye. It was doing a hand-stand and smiling wickedly. Funny how quickly you could get used to weird and impossible things happening all around you. Everything was strangely mixed up. Here he was with an invisible dog, a troll and Fiendish and Lucy. A Lucy who could do magic, so much magic that the garingay wanted to steal her. He wished he could do a little bit of magic himself though the troll did like him, even if he could do no magic at all. Tickles had woken up and was pulling at his shirt. He seemed excited. Lucy had become the old Lucy who used to do star work. She had been smelling that cake for so long that one might think her nose had been made for eating. A large crumb fell on one of the cards lying on the floor. The card showed a vicious Queen of Clubs who was lifting a huge cat, more like a tiger really, and about to put it in something the shape of a bird cage. The queen let go of the cat and grabbed the crumb eagerly. She put it in her mouth and winked. She was very happy and seemed proud of what she had done. Then she disappeared. No, she hadn't quite disappeared. She had just become very, very small. Henry picked up the card to show Lucy. But it was too late. The cake was just going into her mouth, a huge piece of it. And just as he was feeling quite sure that he wouldn't want her to eat it, then it really was too late. Much too late and he knew that he should have done something.

She was chewing it very thoughtfully. Her face hadn't changed that much, only it was tighter. Tighter and becoming smaller. Eagerly, she tried to stuff the rest into her mouth but Fiendish grabbed hold of her. They were on the ground wrestling. Suddenly she let go. She spat out a bit of cake but it was too late. She was shrinking. It happened quickly when he looked back on it, but as it was happening it seemed to be happening slowly. The slowest moments he'd ever had, as if time was something that could be broken up into small pieces. There she was now, only the size of a mouse, both her hands in the air and her long red hair hanging lose.

'Why did you let her eat it?' shouted Fiendish.

'We tried to stop her.' The troll had his eyes on his feet and wasn't looking at her.

'We really did,' said Henry, his thoughts glazing over in a way that didn't make him feel comfortable. They had tried and anyhow it was her own fault. You couldn't stop Lucy. You just couldn't. No. That was the way she was made. He was different.

Where had she gone? He looked all over the floor. There she was. She was standing on some of the cards that Fiendish and the troll had been playing with. She had that proud look in her eye as if she might still be the queen of his bedroom.

'I've shrunk,' she announced. 'I'm no bigger than the Queen of Hearts, but she looks vicious.' She was standing right on the waist of the queen who had two heads, one at the top of the card and one at the bottom. Both heads smiled and winked in a creepy sort of way. 'Well,' said Lucy putting one hand on her hip stretching herself and sticking her nose in the air. 'Well, I've still got my magic. That won't have shrunk. You can't shrink magic.'

That Lucy! Henry wasn't surprised. Now she was pointing at the troll and giggling.

'Is that how you became the smallest troll in the world? I bet it is.'

No taller than a mug or a playing card, she was wagging her finger at the troll.

'I shouldn't have eaten that horrible cake. It tasted disgusting but it made me eat it. Did it make you?'

The troll nodded.

'Thought so,' whispered Lucy.

'Those cakes do that. They make you eat them. Great Grandma Yo Yitsoo makes them. She has been making them since she was a little girl and they get worse and worse and more and more horrible. She leaves bags of them around and then hopes that someone will eat them and grow so small that she can put them in one of her pockets. She has a huge apron all covered in pockets to put any creature in that has shrunk enough that it fits. I didn't become small enough

to fit into one of her pockets so she left me alone, the smallest troll in the world and quite safe until...'

'Until I made up the yo yitsoo,' said a tiny voice very firmly.

'The one who eats trolls for breakfast and wants their guts for garters. Yes, you made him up, but Great Grandma Yo Yitsoo was already there. She was there making her horrible cakes but I'm not sure she was called yo yitsoo. Perhaps you named her as you invented that guy who wanted me for breakfast. Magic can move forwards and backwards so it's really difficult to know what's happened as it keeps changing.'

'Magic,' said Fiendish, 'can do EVERYTHING. It can even do things to the past. It can unravel it like an old pair of socks and put it together in a different kind of way and you don't know what has happened because magic makes you see things differently and sometimes it just leaves you standing somewhere you've never been before.'

'You're telling me,' said Lucy.

She was looking straight up at him, straight up at her brother Henry. That Henry who hadn't stopped her eating the cake. She could tell that he so wished he had. She knew that feeling.

Henry's big hand came down and picked her up and held her close to his face. His nose was roughly the same size as her and his eyes were almost as big as her head. Humongous, he had become humongous. Even his freckles looked like they had needed buckets of paint. Henry kept looking at her.

Lucy didn't move. Just like her to stand like that and look straight at him as if everything were normal.

'I'm smaller than a troll. I'm the smallest girl in the world and I can hide anywhere.'

'Almost anywhere.'

'Could I fit into the pocket on your shirt?'

Fiendish and the troll were looking at her standing there on Henry's hand. They both nodded. Carefully, Henry slid her into his pocket. She was moving about. It was like having a mouse in your pocket. He bent down feeling for Tickles. That dog! It was lying still and flat on the ground. Perhaps it was ashamed. It ought to be. Those horrible cakes. Henry stroked it.

It was weird stroking an invisible dog. He felt it licking his fingers and he could hear it whimpering like it was sorry. He bent down close. It was saying something. Tickles was talking. At first he found it difficult to understand. Its voice came from deep down and the words slid into one another so it sounded like a low growl. Then it became clear. He was talking about a party. The garingay were going to have a party. A pirate party with a ship. A real ship thought Tickles. Perhaps with cannons. Certainly sails, rigging and a lookout. The Chief Garingay, fat as a sausage, huge as a crocodile, with the mane of a lion, the feet of a dinosaur, was going to sit in the lookout so he wouldn't miss anything that was happening. He had always wanted to be a pirate and to sail the seven seas, he said. Everyone could come to his party, but they had to look like pirates. Tickles wanted to go too and, being invisible, he didn't have to wear any pirate clothes.

'I wish I wasn't invisible,' said Tickles. 'But that's the way I am. I'm quite proud of it really, but sometimes, just sometimes, I wish everyone could see me. I would make a good pirate, I would, better than that horrible, fat old and smelly garingay who hasn't a drop of honest pirate blood in him, not a single drop.'

6

The Party

Fat as a crocodile, old and smelly, the Chief Garingay was standing in the lookout at the top of the mast. He was wearing a patch on one eye and held a telescope to the other. The telescope seemed to be aimed at a piece of sky with nothing in it but a cloud. He was steadying it with both hands and did not move. There must be something in that cloud or perhaps he was just trying very hard at being a pirate and thought that this was a pirate thing to do.

Henry had taken a pair of his father's trousers, cut off the bottoms and tied them round his waist with a piece of rope. He had sneaked through the house. There had been that feeling of no one there, a strange silence that makes footsteps echo but at the end of the garden he had found his father, standing on the old swing and swinging with all his might. He was going so high into the air that it looked like he might fly any moment.

He didn't stop when he saw Henry, but shouted. 'Going to the pirate party are you? Well, I would—except I've got things to do. Important things to do. I've got a meeting with Grandpa Yo Yitsoo who's a real devil for doing things properly. There are at least twenty-six reasons why you shouldn't disappoint a yo yitsoo: for one, they can be dangerous. For two, you have no idea how dangerous, no idea at all. I've forgotten all the other reasons. Completely forgotten, and I don't care. I wouldn't give a monkey's fart for all those reasons. All I know is what I know and that's more than enough, thank you. Grandpa Yo Yitsoo and I are going to sit in this garden and make plans.'

'What kind of plans?'

'Wicked plans,' replied his father carelessly bending his legs and disappearing into the air. Henry waited for the swing to return but no, it too had vanished. The garden was empty. In front of him was the wood. The wood was very silent except for a slight rustle in the leaves. The trees seemed to be stretching out their branches to greet him. Yes, they were longer than before and different. They looked like trolls.

In his pocket was his pass. Guest Pass Magic Garden First Order–Admit One. Perhaps using the pass made him see things. Suddenly the swing was back. It came empty through the air and swung back and forth a few times. Then it was still. He could feel Lucy in his shirt pocket. Carefully, he let his fingers find her and took her out.

'Did you hear that?' he whispered. 'Dad is meeting up with Grandpa Yo Yitsoo.'

'Of course I heard that. Haven't gone deaf you know. Just shrunk. Now get on to the party. You don't have to take me out to talk. Just keep rubbing the magic pass with your fingers. That's all that's to it. Easy peasy. But no one else can hear us.'

He hadn't asked her how he was going to find the party. The troll and Fiendish were going to be there. They all seemed to think that he would know how to get there, though neither he nor Lucy had ever been in the wood before. Strange that. But he had found the party without any trouble. It was as if his feet had known the way and now he was there looking up at the Chief Garingay who was in the lookout.

Strange how he had got there. Through the

trees a path had appeared that was always disappearing into a thicker part of the woods, where the branches were much too close for any path. Then, just as you were almost there, almost where the path had vanished a moment before, there it was again, just in front of you. It was a real maze of a path, turning this way and that, forking here and there, branching off one moment and then turning back on itself. He didn't know the way but his feet had just kept going with a strange certainty as if they'd been there before. He trusted them. Lucy had become very still.

Suddenly, as they entered a clearing, there it was, a huge pirate ship surrounded by tall grass. When the wind blew through it, the ship looked like it rode green and yellow waves like a real ship on the high seas. All over the deck and on the rigging there were garingay dressed as pirates. They were easy to recognize because of their scaly legs and huge feet with blue toes. The small hairy things must be trolls and those strange creatures with ears as big as elephant ears and tails like lizards must be yo yitsoo. But he couldn't see Fiendish or the troll with the red hair anywhere. Perhaps they weren't there yet.

The Chief Garingay lowered his telescope and waved both hands in the air. Everyone fell silent and looked up. Something was sniffing Henry's feet. Tickles, it must be Tickles, that clever invisible dog with the six feet. The Chief Garingay coughed very loudly. Henry bent down slowly and felt around by his feet. Yes, it was there and that made him feel just a little safer.

When he looked up, the Chief Garingay was still waving his hands. He noticed that he was now holding a trumpet in one of them. A big shiny trumpet.

'When I blow, anything that is invisible becomes visible!'

He lifted the trumpet and blew. The noise was like wind caught in a sick elephant's trunk. What a rattling sound!

On the ground, right next to Henry was a long, six-legged dog with big eyes.

'I've never tried this before. Never ever tried being visible before. Doesn't feel very different, you know.'

The dog yawned.

The trumpet sounded again. This time it was high and shrill, finishing with a tired squeak. Tickles had disappeared but things weren't back to what they had been before. Not quite. Not when he looked carefully. Some creatures had become strangely bigger. The trolls had bigger heads and longer tails and seemed to glow.

'Aha,' shouted the Chief Garingay. 'Can I see trolls! Can I see trolls!'

He blew again. This time Henry had to hold his ears just to keep standing.

Now the place was completely empty. A strange ghostly emptiness because you could hear the whispering and talking of all the many creatures who were really there. There and all around. Henry didn't dare move. He could see nothing, absolutely nothing, but there must be creatures all around him. Even the pirate ship had vanished. He could hear a voice. The voice came from where the pirate ship had been.

'Somewhere,' said the voice. 'Somewhere there is a girl. A girl called Lucy who has got some magic, lots of magic. More magic than is good for her. More magic than is good for anyone. Ever.' The voice came closer, seeming to float through the air. 'Lucy, I'm coming to get you. I'm coming to get you, Lucy, and I'll take you and all your magic because today is the day when the garingay come to steal you. We can

steal anything. We can even steal the moon, if we want to. Lucy, where are you?'

The voice stopped. Everywhere there was the noise of invisible creatures, yo yitsoo, garingay and trolls. Witches too, perhaps. It was impossible to know what there might be lurking in this wood. Tickles was at his feet. He could feel his invisible tail sweeping across the grass and his tongue licking his feet.

'Tickles,' whispered Henry. 'Tickles.'

'Follow me,' said the dog. 'Follow me and I'll take you to Fiendish and my master, the little troll.'

'But I can't see you!'

'Bend down, just bend down and feel for my tail. Grab it, but you have to be quick.'

Henry could feel the tail. Tickles had very thick fur. It was a good long tail. He had to hold on tight. The dog was running fast and Henry didn't have time to look around. They were back inside the wood but they hadn't gone far. He could still hear all that whispering, talking and shouting and the sound of all those feet. Tickles was sniffing round to find his way. He headed for a dark tunnel of bushes and briars. Henry had to bend down and run at the same time. A branch hit him in the face and he slipped and fell. He let go of the tail and he could hear Tickles running on. The wood had closed all around him. It was getting dark. He felt his pocket. Yes, Lucy was still there. He rubbed the pass so he could hear her from deep inside his pocket.

'Just wait. He'll be back. That dog will be back. I'm hungry. Pick me one of those berries.'

A big raspberry was right above him. He picked it and slipped it into his pocket. He could hear her munching.

'Those garingay. Those stupid garingay. I should never have invented them, but I didn't know what I was doing and it's such fun inventing things. And Fiendish was such a good thing to invent. Such a brilliant, fantastically brilliant thing to invent.'

Suddenly he could see a light. A light coming down the tunnel of briars. There was Fiendish holding a torch and behind him the troll with the red hair. They seemed to be floating on air. Tickles, they must be riding on Tickles. How Henry wished he could ride that dog. To ride an invisible dog, why nothing could be cooler than that. Nothing in the world!

They were waving to him. They wanted him to join them on that long dog, the dog with six legs.

'Hold on!' shouted Fiendish and he did, very tight. The trees flew past him in a rush of green and brown and the air felt cool on his cheeks. He could think of nothing but holding on. The troll was in front, his hair streaming behind him like two flames. Fiendish was holding on to the troll, his back bent over to let the roar of wind flash by. In his pocket he could feel Lucy jumping up and down. She was excited. The wind must be going straight through her, the way it hit him in the chest. This was the best thing he had ever done, beyond anything he could ever have imagined. You didn't ride an invisible six legged dog, not even in your dreams. Not even if you were Henry and could think all sorts of things, more than most people would dare, even when they let their wildest thoughts run loose.

'Be careful,' shouted Fiendish because he had to shout in the rush of wind. 'Be careful of the garingay. You can never trust them, not when the moon is blue.'

There it was, just above the black winter branches of the wood floating in a big sky—a dark blue moon.

'You can't trust anything or anyone. Not when the moon is blue. When it's blue, dark magic creeps into all creatures who know anything about magic, anything at all. Even if they're small.'

'As small as a mouse?'

'Smaller, even smaller than a beetle or spider. Everything is different when the moon is blue. And it's bad luck, fiendishly bad luck that the garingay want to steal Lucy on a night when the moon is blue. It means, it means...'

The rest of what Fiendish was saying was

drowned in the roar of the wind. Henry bent forward so that he was leaning on Tickles' soft invisible back. They had left the wood. How could that wood be so humongous when it didn't look at all big from their garden? Why, they lived in the middle of the city and there was just this little wood behind their garden. It looked big, but their mother was always telling people it was small. 'There's a small wood at the end of our garden,' she would say. 'Really just a couple of trees, only the children think it's so huge they're afraid of getting lost!' And she would laugh. 'Henry says there are trolls in the wood.' And their father might add, even if he must know that no one would listen, 'I can think of twenty-six reasons, twenty-six sensible reasons why trolls don't exist, but Henry doesn't believe a word I say, not a single word.'

But that felt a very long time ago. His mother had seen a garingay and his father had brought a chocolate cake for Grandpa Yo Yitsoo who was a hundred and one today. Now, he went around saying that he knew twenty-six reasons why it's good to know a troll! Lucy had become as small as a mouse and was hiding in his pocket and the moon was blue and he was riding an invisible dog heading for he did not know where while the garingay were having a party, a wild pirate party somewhere in the middle of that wood.

There was something in front of the moon. A tall tower with a huge black bell swinging back and forth but not a sound was heard. Suddenly a cloud of bats flew out from underneath the bell and there was a deafening noise. The tower was standing in a deep field of soft grass and Tickles was heading for it and slowing down.

'We are here,' said a deep voice, which Henry recognized. It was Tickles. What a dog!

'Now we must sit still and wait. We have to wait for the witch, the one who lives in this tower and who only speaks to people once in a while. Once in a very long while.'

'Once in a blue moon,' said the troll. 'That is a piece of luck. Our first piece of luck. Shhh....There she is.'

He was pointing at the tower. And there, swinging on the edge of the bell was a tiny woman, no bigger than a cat. She had a long nose and a pointed hat, just as a witch should. Everything about her was just perfectly witch, even the way she moved. And the way she hung on the very rim of the bell was so awesome that he couldn't take his eyes off her. Between her legs was a broomstick. She was swinging back and forth. Then, as the bell slowed down, she let go and flew through the air, right down to where they were. She stood right close to him, looking straight at his face.

'I've got witch's eyes,' she was saying. 'You can't outstare me, so don't even try.'

A strange silence hung among the trees in the wood.

'I'm Henrietta,' she said. 'I'm a small witch, a very small witch.'

'The smallest in the world?' asked Henry.

'How did you guess?'

'I just knew.'

She smiled. 'I like you,' she said. 'There is something about you even if you haven't got any magic and you are a boy. Well, one must take things as they are, as my grandmother used to say. And was she a witch! A witch and half! But that was many moons ago— green moons, blue moons, enough moons to make your head spin. Back then Tickles was her familiar, before that incy troll came along with his red hair and big ideas. What do you think of him, Tickles the invisible six legged dog?' She stroked the air fondly.

'He's awesome, that dog,' whispered Henry.

'I made him,' said the witch. 'I made him back in the days when I had more magic. He's all that's left of those glory days. Still, it doesn't do to look backwards and I hardly ever do, but he's a fine hound.'

'Awesome.'

'Awesome, my hat, awesome, my broomstick! He's much more than awesome. He's glorious, quite simply glorious and there is no dog like him in the whole world, and do I know the world. I have been east of the sun and west of the moon and as far as that icy place where you only find penguins and seals and the nights are so long that you sometimes think that the sun has been swallowed up by a pitchy sea of darkness that ain't going to spit it out again, not ever.'

She was exactly the same height as he was but everything about her was small except her broomstick, which was much too big.

'I borrowed it,' she said. 'Really, I found it and finders keepers. Isn't it fiendishly cool? It was made for a much bigger witch, back in the days when there were bigger witches. Now they're all disgustingly small, like me. It's the cakes, of course. Grandma Yo Yitsoo's delicious, scrum-diddly magical cakes, they've made almost all of us smaller here in this glorious and fantastic wood. What do you think, boy?' She had lost her breath and had to stop. 'Impressed? Admit you are impressed. Admit your brain is spinning so that you don't know what to think. Why look at you, perfectly clueless! You don't know how to speak to a witch, never mind a yo yitsoo or garingay. Now let me tell you: always say the first thing that enters your head. That's hardly ever wrong, not if you have a good head. Never say the second thing. That's bound to wind someone up and you don't want to do that, not if you're speaking to someone who has magic, pure magic and at their fingertips.' She snapped her fingers. 'My fingers can do anything, and believe me they have.'

She had a huge smile and a greedy pair of eyes. They were so big that he could see the varied flecks of colour clearly: green, yellow, grey and brown surrounding a centre of dead black. They didn't have an ordinary way of looking. Those eyes saw everything and took notes.

'You are coming close to outstaring me,' she said. 'Closer than anyone has before, ever. A boy like you might even be allowed to ride on my broomstick. Wow! And you're the son of the guy who was always going around saying that he could think of twenty-six reasons why trolls don't exist! Mind you, he doesn't say that anymore. Now he's busy wishing that they really didn't exist and that this place wasn't full of magic to burst.' She laughed and putting one hand (how long her fingers were and how quick) on his shoulder, she leaned forwards till she almost touched his face. 'I can tell you he's regretting it. Those twenty-six reasons! I bet he wishes he had them all in a box and could throw them down a well or flush them down a toilet for making him look so stupid. But that's too late. Much too late.'

Her voice had become a whisper and the tip of her nose was touching his cheek. 'Much too late. Grandpa Yo Yitsoo has turned him into something weird and wonderful and keeps him in a cage like a familiar.'

'He's turned him into WHAT?'

'No idea. Looks a bit like a pelican to me.'

'A pelican!'

'I said 'a bit like'. Some kind of bird, anyhow. He's got a beak. A beak and a half—so you say to yourself 'pelican' before you have even had time to look at the rest. The rest isn't perhaps that much pelican, come to think of it.'

She put one finger to her forehead and scratched 'The rest is …let me see…more fox, I would say. Fox, squirrel or weasel perhaps. Something like that, something small, quick and rapacious. Do you know that word? It's a good word, really cool. It means something that

101

snatches and grabs with all the wildness of a tiger, the greed of an elephant and knows how to bite. Anyhow, he's in a cage and Grandpa Yo Yitsoo is heading for that pirate party, cage in hand, strutting proudly as if he owned the world. That will teach your dad never to have twenty-six reasons for anything, least of all that there are no trolls—no trolls anywhere in the whole world!'

'Has he really become a sort of cross between a pelican and a weasel or a fox?'

'You bet!' Laughed the witch.

She sat down and undid her shoes. 'Sorry,' she said, 'but my toes must have air. They need to breathe, you know, before there's any action.'

She had her legs spread out and was wiggling her toes. 'Bats like my toes because they can feel the magic. Just look at them circling round my feet. They live in my belfry and they like to go wherever I go and I don't mind, they can please themselves, they can. Don't you agree, Henry? Bet you do. I can feel that you've got attitude.'

'How did you know my name?'

'Fiendish told me. He said, 'I've got a new friend called Henry. Small fellow, not much to look at, smells too, but he understands. He understands the wood and all its magic even if he hasn't got any himself.'

They were siting next to each other, Fiendish, the troll, the witch and Henry and inside Henry's pocket was Lucy. In front of them lay Tickles and the witch was stroking him with one foot while she held the other very still, to encourage any bats who might be too shy to explore her toes otherwise.

Behind them was the tower. Below, the meadow slopped towards a ring of tall dark trees. In the sky was a huge blue moon, not quite full and streaked with red, as if on fire.

'Time to go,' said the witch kicking her feet so that the bats flew up. 'Time to go and join the party. I do love parties because we do such wonderful parties, not like human parties. Human parties, you go and come back yourself. Here you never know. You don't know anything at all, Henry. You just have to be prepared. You can be turned into something that's a bit like a pelican and end up in a cage at the drop of a wild bit of magic. Where's your sister by the way? She's become so wonderfully wicked, that kid who used to do star work for mummy! Where is she?'

'In my pocket.'

'Hope she isn't squished!'

Henry lifted her out and held her out on his hand. Did she stand proud!

'Oh dear,' shouted the witch and grabbed her. 'You shouldn't do that! One of the bats might get her and fly away you never know where. They're dangerous are bats because they'll work for anyone and they spy like mad. I don't mind them on my toes but I wouldn't trust them, not for anything. She's better in my big apron pocket. It's full of room and there are a few scrumdiddly bits floating about for her to eat.'

She looked at Henry. 'I know what you are thinking, but you can trust me. There is nothing in my pocket that'll harm Lucy. I'll give you a witch's word— by the deepest magic known and brewed, by all creatures of this wood that fly, crawl or creep, I Henrietta, the smallest witch in the world, do swear that I won't tell Henry any lies, not a single porky pie not now or ever, unless he decides to do star work or some other silly thing to impress some human, here there or anywhere, east of the sun and west of the moon. Well, will that do?'

For a moment Henry didn't know what to say, but then they all began to laugh, a warm trickle of laughter. First Fiendish laughed, then the troll, and from somewhere in the meadow he could hear Tickles yelping with laughter and then the tiny laughter of his sister Lucy from inside the deep pocket of the witch who was looking at him very seriously.

'Not a single porky, but we're in a hurry. The moon only stays blue for a little while and is gone in a bat's wink or the cough of a snail. It can never do to be late—and I never am. I can't be, there's such a tingling in my spine that I'm always in a fearful rush.'

But no one moved. They were waiting for something.

'The dog,' said the witch. 'There is something that dog hasn't told me. I can tell, Tickles. Spit it out!'

And he heard Tickle's growly voice. 'She has invented them. Lucy has invented the yo yitsoo and the garingay and …'

'She hasn't invented me,' interrupted the witch. 'You couldn't invent me. I'm just too evil, too perfectly, wickedly evil for that. But the garingay and the yo yitsoo! There was always something a bit invented about them, but now it's official. Bet that has really wound them up!'

'They don't mind or they pretend not to mind. No one likes being invented. But that's their tough luck, but that's not all, because just as one can remember and one can forget...'

'I understand,' whispered the witch.

'There is always an opposite.'

'Sometimes a dangerous opposite.'

'One can invent and un-invent,' bellowed Fiendish. They could feel the ground shaking as he jumped up and down with excitement. 'I never thought of that. Never, ever, not till I heard Grandpa Yo Yitsoo say it.'

Silence, and all around them that wood and above them, the blue moon, that blue ghostly moon. There must be so much magic lurking everywhere.

'That's what they deserve, those horrible yo yitsoo who eat trolls for breakfast and want their guts for garters,' shouted Henry.

'Garters,' echoed the wood, and from deep among the trees came a sudden rush of ice-cold wind.

'Come,' whispered Fiendish. 'We must go but I bet you can do it Lucy, I bet you can.' He didn't sound so sure.

'Do what?'

'Un-invent.'

They got back onto Tickles. Everything seemed to be flying past them as they sped through the wood. Henry was sitting in front. He could feel the bony hands of the witch digging into him and holding on.

7

A Pelican Fox

Suddenly Tickles stopped and began sniffing the ground.

'Getting closer. Fee-fi-fo-fum I can smell all those garingay and yo yitsoo. And now I think I can hear them—what a party.'

The witch let go of Henry and scratched her nose with one hand. With the other she lifted up her skirt and gave it a shake. A bat flew out and hung in the air facing them. It had made slits of its eyes and its face was scrunched up. It looked embarrassed. It turned and fluttered towards the wood like a black handkerchief in the air.

'Bloody spy,' snorted the witch. 'You can hardly breathe for spies in this wood.'

'We'll be there soon,' said Tickles. 'You need to be prepared. There is nothing in the world those garingay want more than to steal Lucy and that would be horrible. Think what would happen...'

'It wouldn't be as bad as stealing me!' laughed the witch.

'Wouldn't it?' said Fiendish slowly. 'Think about it. If they stole her magic, all the creatures they could invent—it would be enough to scare the pants off a dinosaur or a small troll or a very small witch!'

'All the creatures they could invent,' said the little witch dreamily. 'Oh, how I would like your magic, Lucy! There has never been magic like it, not ever. How did you find it?'

'I don't know,' came Lucy's voice from deep inside the witch's pocket. 'I suppose it was just there, and so was I.'

'All the best magic is like that, just there waiting for someone to find it. It's been like that as far back as anyone can remember, as far back as those woolly mammoths who lived with trolls in caves. Every now and then, wandering on one of those endless plains the world used to be so full of, they would find some magic which they didn't know what to do with so they would just take it in their trunks and give it to trolls, but no one does that any more, gives magic away—no one in their right mind. It's something that you keep and hoard,' said the troll. 'And take out on rainy days and look at when you are all on your own so that no one, but no one can touch it. Only the yo yitsoo are careless about magic. They're dripping in it and don't care at all. They put it in cakes if they feel like it or leave it hanging from their tails for anyone to steal, but you have to be careful. You never know what you have got your hands on, like those cakes that made me small or whatever has turned your dad into a pelican of sorts.'

They heard a large bang and a burst of stars filled the sky. The fireworks had begun. Everyone would be staring at those fireworks. A perfect time to arrive.

Suddenly they could see the tall masts of the pirate ship. Silently they split into twos. Tickles and the troll, Lucy and the witch, Henry and Fiendish. At the stroke of midnight, the witching hour, they would meet again in Henry's bedroom—if they were still enough themselves to do that.

'You never know,' said the witch. 'Not when it's a blue moon!'

They moved across the cold wet grass, heading for the huge hull of the pirate ship. Just below the blue moon, a couple of bats were winging their way.

'Beware of spies,' whispered the witch. 'Never, ever trust a bat—not even in a moment of danger and nowhere else to turn, or you'll live to regret it!'

When she reached the pirate ship, the witch climbed up like a squirrel in a tree. Her long fingers and toes found cracks between the planks everywhere and within seconds she had reached the railing. Fiendish was right behind. She waited for a burst of fireworks before she slid onto the deck. It was packed with garingay, yo yitsoo and trolls, all of them with their eyes on the sky. The smoke had blotted out the moon and the ring of dark trees. Thousands of stars came tumbling down, each with a wiggling tail of fire, mingling in one thick mass of flashing lights and streams of burning colours. Stars were vanishing one after the other, but new ones kept appearing. At first, the stars were winning, but then the darkness began to swell like a wave. Fewer stars were coming. They winked timidly and had shorter tails and the darkness grew and grew. It was a strange darkness, not like any Henry knew. It seemed to slide along like a wave of something thick and sticky, covering everything completely.

Slowly, he began to climb the side of the ship.

His hands and feet searched for places to hold onto, but it was difficult and the ship was so tall, a dark looming height. When he was almost half way, he saw for a moment the witch peering over the railing. Then the swish of a rope hit him in the face. He grabbed it. Swinging from side to side, holding on tight, he managed to climb up on deck.

'Never thought you were going to make it!' whispered the witch. 'And we don't have time to spare. Look, that darkness will soon finish off the moon.'

The moon was still there but almost everything else had been swallowed up. The boat was standing in a cold sea of night and the ground below was black and endless. All around him, garingay and yo yitsoo were jumping up and down, all excited about the last fireworks. They were gabbling like mad and took no notice of anyone around them except to push and nudge. Some of them had small shiny trumpets with a strange rusty sound that lingered in the air long after they'd been blown. There was a stamping and a clapping. The Chief Garingay had come down from his lookout and was standing by the ship's wheel with Grandpa Yo Yitsoo. They were talking about something and shouting, but in the general roar Henry couldn't hear a word. Next to Grandpa Yo Yitsoo was a tall birdcage. Inside was a weird looking creature that was part pelican. It had the head of a pelican; a sad looking big eyed pelican while the rest was something else, something with a tail and claws. Badger or fox, the witch had said. Whatever it was jumped up and down and seemed to be waving at Henry. Where was Lucy?

'Still in my pocket,' said the witch. 'She's almost become my familiar. She's stuffed herself on purple berries and gone to sleep but I'm going to wake her up. She's no bigger than a mouse and would fit inside the pocket of Grandpa Yo Yitsoo's trousers. And they'll all be looking for her and trying to steal her! What fun!'

Henry couldn't take his eyes off the pelican with a tail and furry behind. It too was looking at him. It winked. Henry winked back. Something very small was scuttling along the deck heading for Grandpa Yo Yitsoo. Among all the shadows it was impossible to see what it was. It could be a mouse or some weird beetle. But when it began to climb up Grandpa Yo Yitsoo's trousers, one could see it was human. Very small, but clearly human.

'Uh, I can feel something,' said Grandpa Yo Yitsoo. 'Something is tickling me—how dare it!' He felt his bottom carefully. 'That tickler is going to come to a sticky end. It feels like a mouse. Yum, yum—I shall have it for dinner. Yummy, yummy dinner...'

His hand moved down towards his pocket. His big hairy thumb almost touched Lucy as she jumped inside.

Henry began to move slowly towards the cage. He tried to hide behind a tall garingay who was busy talking to Grandpa Yo Yitsoo. The cage was right in front of him and the pelican was looking him straight in the face.

'Look what has happened to me,' whispered the pelican fox looking around nervously. 'I was all friendly with that guy, Grandpa Yo Yitsoo. Even brought him a cake, and look what he's done. Gave me a weird cup of something green I just couldn't resist — seconds later I was in this cage. You can't trust anyone here. They're weird and wicked and I should NEVER have entered this wood. I can tell you twenty-six reasons why not: first, they've got all the magic in the world. Second, you never know what they are going to do with it. Third, when you *do* know it's too late, much too late...'

But Henry had put his fingers in his ears and wasn't listening.

'Shut up,' said Grandpa Yo Yitsoo and kicked the cage. 'I have had enough of your twenty-six reasons. Who were you talking to anyway? No one here would listen to you!'

'No one, I was talking to no one at all. I was just keeping myself company, talking to myself,' said the pelican sadly. 'I don't think anyone is ever going to listen to me again. Not ever.'

'Quite right,' said Grandpa Yo Yitsoo. 'No one is ever going to listen to you again. I don't think anyone ever did. My kind of magic doesn't always last forever. There is a way of undoing it, but I don't think you ever will.'

'How?' asked the pelican hopefully.

'All you have to do is find someone who can remember all of your twenty-six reasons why there are no trolls and can recite them without falling asleep or laughing. All the trolls know them but they laugh themselves silly do trolls just thinking of you, never mind the twenty-six reasons.'

'What about Lucy or Henry?'

'No chance! Lucy might remember six, but Henry!'

'One or two if I'm lucky.'

A big tear rolled down the cheek of the pelican. 'Oh, the wicked, wicked trolls! I should never ever had said that there are twenty-six reasons why trolls don't exist!'

'Too late,' laughed Grandpa Yo Yitsoo and kicked the cage so that it rolled along the deck. 'Much, much too late and serve you right, you silly billy man! Now the moon is blue and you are going to see more magic than you have had hot dinners.' He rubbed his big paws together and jumped up and down. 'And you'll discover that there is more magic in the world than there are stars in the universe, and some of it is scrumdiddlyumptious and wild and funny, and some will make your hair stand on end and your heart beat as if it had gone mad and couldn't take any more.' He put the trumpet to his mouth and blew a long shrill note.

'So there!' He stamped his foot. 'So there! I'm on my way, I am. I don't like parties. They're noisy and silly and full of young yo yitsoo and garingay having fun and I can't stand that, I really can't. It makes me so angry I want to shout and scream, I do.' He swung the cage back and forth.

'I'm leaving my new familiar, the guy who

used to have twenty-six reasons for everything and who is now a pelican, and I think a fox, though I'm not too sure. I think the back bit is fox. I was going to make it an anteater. I just love anteaters but then just as I was going to say 'anteater' I changed my mind and out came 'fox.' Well, I'm going to go to the captain's room and read some books on magic and, if you're all good, I might do one or two tricks before that blue moon has vanished from the sky.' Grandpa Yo Yitsoo put the cage down.

'So that's what I am,' whispered the creature sadly. 'A cross between a pelican and a fox! Well, with that funny tail, I expected as much. Comes as no surprise really, but he could show a little more respect, just a weeny bit. Not a lot to ask when you are sitting in a cage and have been treated this badly!'

Grandpa Yo Yitsoo climbed down the stairs just behind the Chief Garingay. The last thing Henry saw was his big bottom with its two pockets. A small hand was waving at him from one of the pockets.

'If that isn't Henry!' shouted one of the trolls. 'Welcome to our party! Isn't it funny that your dad has been turned into fox and a pelican? Just what he always deserved. Something big and silly that people can't help staring at, him and his twenty-six reasons! But I like you. We all like you. You're the only one who always believed in trolls. You just knew that they were real but you didn't believe in garingay or yo yitsoo. Well, everyone makes a mistake and, anyway they're made up. It's twice as difficult to believe in something that's made up. At least twice as difficult or maybe even three times as difficult, so we'll let you off. But your dad with his twenty-six reasons! He deserves to be a pelican fox and can stay that forever and ever and ever, till there are cows on the moon.'

The cage had rolled along the deck till it reached a coil of rope not far from them. The Chief Garingay looked at it, raised his eyebrows and laughed. The pelican fox was lying on its side, its feathers all a mess. It got up, shook itself and stamped.

'I can think of twenty-six reasons,' shouted the pelican fox. 'Twenty-six reasons why I don't want to be a pelican fox. For one, I don't really know what to EAT. I don't think I like ANYTHING. Grandpa Yo Yitsoo has been giving me all sorts of ants: yellow ants, red ants, black ants. I CAN-NOT STAND ANTS. I am NOT an anteater, will you please! I've got the behind of a fox, and a fine fox too and the head of a pelican, an ancient and venerable bird. I deserve some respect, but I don't know what to eat. I don't think I like raw fish.' The pelican fox became thoughtful. 'Or perhaps I do,' it added sadly. 'There is perhaps something scrumdiddlyumptious about a wiggly waggly fish.'

'Shut up,' shouted up a small troll.

'A wiggly waggly fish jumping around in my beak! Why I could think of twenty-six reasons why...'

'Not twenty-six reasons!'

One of the trolls took the cage and let it drop over the side of the ship. It landed with a big thud. The pelican fox jumped up and down.

'I won't have it!' shouted the pelican fox. 'I won't be put in a stupid cage by silly trolls and treated like this! It just isn't fair!'

'Losers aren't choosers,' laughed a troll.

And another, 'I know twenty-six reasons why he'll never get out of that cage!'

'Look,' an old garingay with a white beard was pointing at the cage. 'Look, in a few minutes the light of the moon is going to hit that cage!'

Just then the light of the moon fell on the ship,

an eerie blue grey light which made everything stand out as if it had been drawn with a thick pen. The wrinkled face of the garingay who was pointing at the cage seemed etched onto the night. The two masts loomed taller and darker. A strange howl was coming from the wood, the sound of an animal or an angry wind. Everyone seemed to know what was happening but Henry was on his own. Tickles might be close by, but he was invisible. There were strange creatures all around him and he didn't like the way their eyes were on him in the blue light and how they'd all stopped talking. There was something by his feet. Slowly his fingers searched the air. Something soft met the touch, that dog. He buried his fingers in its invisible coat. He looked up. The witch Henrietta was sitting on the heavy cross beam swinging her legs, next to her was Fiendish. They were all silently looking at the wood.

'I can think of twenty-six reasons why I don't want to be a pelican with the behind of a fox,' came an angry voice from somewhere not far away. 'I can think of twenty-six very good reasons:

1. Their beaks are much too big.
2. I don't like the way they fly.
3. They're more like dinosaurs than birds.

4. They eat only fish.
5. They eat them whole, head tail and all.
6. They wiggle as they slip down your throat.
7. And jump about in your pouch.'

The voice began to slow down. 'I never ever wanted to be a pelican. Not ever.'

It became thoughtful and sad. 'And a pelican with the furry behind of a fox— a great bushy tail! Foxes are fine creatures, but the behind of a fox and the head of a pelican!'

A shadow emerged from the woods; an enormous hand picked up the cage and shook it. Whoever owned that hand was so huge its shadow rolled like a sea across the field. Henry didn't dare look up. The shadow was enough.

'It's Grandma Yo Yitsoo,' whispered Tickles. 'She appears now and again, once in a blue moon and she's the only thing that's really big around here. So many of us are small having tried her cakes. They're just too tempting. And she's made herself bigger, I don't know how. Probably she's eaten some kind of berries or just picked up some magic somewhere. She's bad,' continued Tickles. 'But she ain't evil. She's put your father back down on the deck having smelled him. She smells everything. Her nose is fantastic but her eyes and ears aren't so good. She won't have been invited to the party. No one ever invites her but if the moon is blue she always turns up and then there is trouble, big trouble.' Tickles became silent. The shadow kept growing.

'I can think of twenty-six reasons,' shouted the pelican fox. 'Twenty-six reasons why I think you are all disgustingly rude. No one here has any manners. Why someone just poked a huge nose into my cage and sniffed me, stuck out a tongue, laughed a horrible laugh and put me down again. Is that manners? Is that how to behave, is that etiquette? I would like to know!'

'What's etiquette?' asked Tickles. 'Never heard that word before and I have heard all sorts of things. Sometimes my ears feel like dropping off because they've just heard too much. Them woolly mammoths never heard of etiquette, nor have trolls.'

'It's a stupid word for manners and being polite. When he gets excited my dad uses funny words and gets all tangled up in his reasons.'

'I smell what I like,' boomed a voice above them. 'What I like, when I like. I can do whatever I like. I'm Grandma Yo Yitsoo and I may have been invented, but I stand tall and firm on two legs and I do what I like and I've got more magic than anyone here. Where is that little girl, that Lucy who had the gumption to invent most of you? I would like to meet you, Lucy,' the voice was trying to sound warm. 'I would really like to meet you Lucy. The things the two of us could do together! Why it would take your breath away!'

Henry looked up. Above him he saw a huge face, green eyed, wrinkled and thick lipped. The lips were moving slowly, very slowly. 'LU-CY, come here Lucy. Oh Lucy. Together we might invent a new universe of creatures.' The face closed its eyes. It was dreaming, imagining, tasting a wonderful future. 'A new universe. Not since the dinosaurs…'

Henry locked his fingers into Tickles' warm fur.

'The garingay promised me that they would steal you,' whispered Grandma Yo Yitsoo to herself. 'They did promise, they really did. And a promise is a promise or I'm not Grandma Yo Yitsoo.'

Her big face was just above them, but she wasn't looking. She was too busy talking to herself.

'A promise is a promise. They told me. They said, 'we'll catch her and then we'll have a pirate party, a really good party with fireworks.' I hate fireworks because they are so smelly, but I said I would come after the party was over. The moon will be blue I said. That's the best time for magic and you'll always find me there when it's a blue moon. That moon is just so wonderfully wicked and I can feel the magic in my finger tips, it's there pricking away. It's just too delicious.'

Her green eyes were looking straight at him but they didn't see anything. Grandma Yo Yitsoo was in a world of her own.

'I've never known them not do it. Those garingay. They once stole the horns off all the unicorns. They're born stealers. They've got stealing in their blood, so wonderfully wickedly that you just can't believe it. They're the best thieves the world has ever known, from way back when the first creepy crawly made its way across the face of the earth, when the place was nothing but mud and water, water and mud, slime and slugs and other weird and fantastical things that first drew breath when the planet was new and magic hadn't even been invented. No one had even thought of it. They just did things slowly in a creepy and slimy sort of way, but stealing? Why, living creatures have been into that from the very first and getting better at it ever since. Then along came the garingay and that was pure magic…'

'Stealing,' shouted the pelican fox. 'What did you say about stealing?'

'Wasn't talking to you. Don't ever want to talk to you. You're the one with the twenty-six reasons.'

'Can you remember them?' asked the pelican fox hopefully. 'The twenty-six reasons why trolls don't exist?'

'But they do. Trolls do exist. No one even invented them. Why should I remember your reasons? No one ever listened. You just talked, on and on.'

'I'll never be anything but a pelican with the tail of a fox and in a cage! That's just too terrible and all because no one can remember my twenty-six reasons.'

In the dark, Henry could just make out that the pelican fox had gone into a huddle on the bottom of the cage. Its long bushy fox tail lay curled round its beak. Henry tried but he couldn't get any further than reason number six: 'trolls don't exist because they've got tails but no fur, only hair. All mammals with tails are furry.' He was a little unsure of reason three which went something like, when you know an animal, you know what it likes and some of the things it might do. Even a human animal. But you never know where you are with trolls. 'No animal,' he had said very slowly in that way he had when he knew. 'No animal is like that. You always know where you are, just a little bit. But not with trolls—because they're made up.'

'Perhaps trolls aren't like any other animals or creatures.'

'Impossible,' his father had said.' Everything is a bit like something else. If trolls aren't like anything else, then they don't exist.' And his father had smiled. A big patient smile. Then he had gone on with his reasons but Henry hadn't listened.

He felt a bit sorry for him as he lay huddled there, his big pelican eyes fixing the sky with a wild, hopeless stare, his long tail between his thin fox legs.

'I'm sorry,' he whispered. 'And now I know that trolls do exist. They have tails, but no fur and they're completely crazy, stark raving mad and you never know what a troll might do, but they exist, boy do they exist. And anyone who thinks they don't, should keep that to him himself or he'll really wish he'd never heard the word 'troll'.' The pelican fox sighed and a big tear rolled down its feathery cheek.

Grandma Yo Yitsoo bent down and picked up the cage. She held it very close to her face.

'Humans are just so weird,' she said. 'Really, really weird.'

She stuck one of her big nails in the cage and prodded the pelican who made himself even smaller.

'I brought you an incy fish.' Grandma Yo Yitsoo took something out of one of her pockets and stuck it in the cage. Then she put the cage down on the deck of the ship.

'Now where is Lucy?' She lowered her head and now her shadow covered the ship like a black cape. Henry held Tickles close. Someone was coming up from behind them.

'It's me,' whispered Fiendish. 'Me and the smallest troll in the world. Henrietta the witch is just above on the crossbeam. The bats have been working their socks off spying. They know just about everything there is to know.'

Henry looked up at the big crossbeam. In the pale blue moonlight, he could see a swarm of bats slowly circling Henrietta. Four of them landed on her outstretched hands fixing their eyes on her. She was holding the bats close to her face. He could hear them whispering.

'What's going on?' shouted Grandma Yo Yitsoo. 'What are you gibbering and jabbering about, you silly bats? Talk louder, I'm quite deaf!'

Henry could hear Fiendish and the little troll with red hair laughing quietly.

'No one laughs at me,' boomed Grandma Yo Yitsoo. 'And anyone who does, I shall make so small,' she squeezed her eyelids together. 'So small that I can squish and squash them between my finger nails like a flea.' She lifted her huge hands above her head closing her fingers, nails tight together. 'Squish , squash, all gone!'

She began to dance, a strange whirling dance, and her shadow shot up and down the deck.

'The moon is blue, bright blue. And wickedness is in the air.' She was shouting, clapping her hands and stamping her big hairy feet. 'Just give me Lucy's magic. Just let my hands close on that wee human child.'

'Then what will you do?' asked Fiendish.

'Take away her magic and put her in a box! I'll invent creatures the world has never seen and no has ever thought of, or could think of. Creatures with eyes in their tummies and ears on their toes and who catch things with their tails. Creatures who can smell if someone farts somewhere across the world and who can read people's thoughts even before they've done the thinking! It will be fantastical and so wicked, it'll blow you away. The world will be mine, I tell you! And I'll invent something even more fiendish than Fiendish, even trollier than trolls, even more witchy than witches. But I want her now, because the moon

is blue and that's the best time for magic there ever, ever was.'

Again she clapped and danced round the ship, a wobbly dance, like a jelly on legs. Henry looked up and there it hung —a blue, bat streaked moon looking down at him with its cold eerie eye. All around them everyone was talking and shouting just as before and two small trolls were handing out fireworks. The witch Henrietta was standing on tiptoes on the crossbeam then she let herself fly. As she came close to the deck, she grabbed hold of one of the ropes dangling down from the crossbeam. She swung through the air and her toes almost grazed his head. Down she jumped.

'The bats say Lucy is deep down in the boat with Grandpa Yo Yitsoo, Henry. Some of them are keeping an eye on her. They like her—she's cool and wild is Lucy, the Lucy who knows magic.'

'Can you trust a bat?'

'You can't trust anyone or anything when the moon is blue and the world is just bursting with magic but the bats don't like Grandma Yo Yitsoo and they think Lucy's cool.'

Henrietta put her broom between her legs and swung herself into the air.

8

The best magic comes last!

Grandpa Yo Yitsoo had gone down into the captain's room in the hope of finding some really good books on magic. He had a secret wish to do even better magic than Grandma Yo Yitsoo. They had been competing for as long as they had known each other.

'I'm not going to be defeated!' He kept whispering to himself. 'Not by that grumpy old so and so who is always making those horrible cakes that no one can resist and who has made herself so big that she looks like a balloon with arms and legs. She's got one of the best noses in the world but she is as deaf as a post while I can hear a mouse squeak.'

This wasn't true, fortunately for Lucy who was still in his pocket.

'It's a blue moon and they don't come very

often. Well, only once in a blue moon! And when the moon is blue you can do at least twice as much magic as a good witch can do when she's trying her very best and is cross-eyed with the effort. Yes, one has to grab a blue moon when it's there because you never know when it's going to happen again. I'm a hundred and one and it could be another hundred years till we have a blue moon so I'm not letting that chance slip by.'

It was very dark in the captain's room and Grandpa Yo Yitsoo only had one candle so he didn't notice all the bats that had followed him and who were sitting all around, all folded up like small umbrellas but their ears wide open. No animal can hear better than a bat. They have got special ears to make up for their eyes that are almost blind. So there they were, sitting all around him listening to him talk, their faces hidden so he wouldn't see them.

'It's a really funny and rum old place,' said Grandpa Yo Yitsoo looking round. 'Really weird. Those garingay! Some of them must have been down here. They have left what looks like tiny black umbrellas. Paper they must be, some kind of decoration, no use against the rain and black serviettes all over the place. What a mess!'

The bats sat very still and just listened.

'Well I'm going to take down a book and read.'

Behind him was a tall bookcase full of very old leather books, black and green with gold writing. Grandpa Yo Yitsoo took out one, blew a cloud of dust off it and put it down on a table. Then he began reading. He didn't notice that he had one bat sitting on each shoulder or that something the size of a mouse had climbed out of his pocket, up his back and was now on the brim of his hat, holding on with her hands, eyes on the book.

'How to do the most horrible, snorrible magic,' read Grandpa Yo Yitsoo very slowly because he wasn't good at reading and therefore had to do it out loud. 'Different kinds of magic. Magic for bad wizards, worse wizards and those who aren't wizards at all. Magic for those who believe in magic and those who don't believe in magic. Magic for dark nights, stormy nights, nights that are so full of howling that you can't hear your own spells, magic for blue moons, white moons, green and purple moons and when the moon is just a slip of a thing in the sky. Fearsome magic, awesome magic and just magic for a rainy day, to while the time away. I-have-got-nothing-better-to-do magic and magic that does your head in.' Grandpa Yo Yitsoo sighed.

'I just don't know what to choose. It's certainly doing my head in. But the moon is blue and I'm going to beat that old lady, Grandma Yo Yitsoo at magic or my name isn't Grandpa Yo Yitsoo which it is, no doubt about it. She never stops going on about her cakes. So she's shrunk a few trolls and witches but the rest of us aren't nearly as impressed as she thinks. No way! That silly old bat with the big nose.' Grandpa Yo Yitsoo read on. 'Magic tricks for witches and yo yitsoo'. That is me. 'Easy tricks for yo yitsoo.' I'm not doing that. It'll be boring, snoring. 'Difficult tricks for grumpy, difficult witches.' Know a few of them. 'Impossible magic for really clever yo yitsoo and wizards who have their wits about them and stars in their eyes.' Now it's getting better and hotter. 'Magic of invention and un-invention.' Now whatever is that? 'How to make up creatures and unmake them.' Doesn't make sense.' Grandpa Yo Yitsoo looked up at the ceiling thoughtfully. 'Now what shall I do?'

'Do?' whispered the bats.

'Someone is talking to me,' whispered Grandpa Yo Yitsoo. 'How spooky. What can that be? No one here but me. So it must be the book. Magical books often do talk, it's part of their magic. So I'll listen. What are you saying, book?'

Silence.

'Speak!' shouted Grandpa Yo Yitsoo banging the table angrily. 'Speak, silly book.'

'Go to invent and uninvent,' whispered a small girl, the size of a mouse.

'Funny, that sounded like it came from my hat.' He took off his hat but before he had put it on the table Lucy had jumped down onto his shoulder.

'Only a special person can invent and uninvent,' read Grandpa Yo Yitsoo. 'What a load of rubbish! I don't believe that.' He continued, 'the same person must do both things.' Well that makes sense, kind of. 'The person must be human.' How disgusting! 'And come from a family where at least one person absolutely and completely does not believe in magic.' Very rare that, I bet. 'Absolutely and completely. Such a person will hate magic.'

'How can you hate something you don't believe in? Doesn't make sense to me, but the book is talking about humans. Humans can perhaps do that. They do so much that makes no sense. No sense at all. Take that silly man with the twenty-six reasons!'

Grandpa Yo Yitsoo was silent for a moment,

then his eyes grew big. 'Now I get it,' he whispered wiping his brow with a bat he mistook for a black serviette. 'Now I get it. The book is talking about that girl, Lucy.' Slowly he read on. 'To uninvent the person who has this special and rare magic must stand in the lookout post of a ship facing a blue moon and say the words 'rim ram rum, fire and snow, ice and sun by the magic that's begun, let night and air dissolve whoever I name. Let them be gone. Rim ram rum.'

That is silly. Funny, all that reading has done something to my head. I think I can remember the twenty-six reasons. And without thinking, he began in a dreamy sort of voice as if he didn't quite understand what he was saying:

'You only find them in books.

Or stories.

No one has ever seen one.

They are crazy and unpredictable.

They can do anything.

They have tails but no fur.

They come from Norway but hardly ever speak Norwegian.

They live in dark gloomy caves.

Or woods.

But they never leave foot prints,

In fact, no one has ever seen a trace of a troll.

Not anywhere.

Not ever.

Though people claim to have seen all sorts of things: like monsters in lakes.

Witches all over the world.

Fairies too.

Little people.

Dragons.

Talking fish.

Fire in the sky.

Ghosts.

Giant Snowmen.

Leprechauns.

Ghost ships.

Wizards.

In fact, there is no end to the crazy things people say they've seen, but no one has ever seen a troll. Not even a small one.'

Those were his twenty-six reasons. Perfectly good reasons perhaps if it weren't for the fact that trolls do exist. They've been around for thousand and thousands of years and, as some of them are always telling me, they were there in the time of the woolly mammoths who used to lie in their caves snuggled up to trolls listening to their stories. They were there before all of us, and before humans too. This planet has always been full of trolls; it's a troll-infested place though they tend to keep to themselves. I'm not sure why. They're not shy. No, you couldn't call them shy. They're what you would call elusive.' He paused and explained to himself, 'that means they slip through your fingers, disappear when you think you've caught one out of the corner of your eye. Yes, trolls are here one minute and the next— well, gone. Completely gone. Vanished without trace. It's the way they are and they won't change. Not in a million years.'

Grandpa Yo Yitsoo scratched his head and picked his nose thoughtfully. He could hear that something was happening up on deck. There was a loud thump followed by a shout. He couldn't quite hear what it was that was being shouted but he could make out the words 'twenty-six reasons' and 'finally out of that bloody cage.'

'The world,' whispered Grandpa Yo Yitsoo dreamily, 'would be a much worse place without trolls, but try explaining that to humans. They just don't understand. They can't deal with anything that's here one moment and gone the next, bless them.' He blew out the candle. 'No, they can't and so they go around saying that trolls don't exist.'

He got up and closed the book. The place was completely dark but Grandpa Yo Yitsoo had eyes that could see a bit in the dark, not perfectly but well enough. Well enough to make his way upstairs to where they were all making whoopee and dancing about. He could hear the stamping, the tripping, the dancing, the leaping of hundreds of feet. Hundreds of garingay, yo yitsoo and trolls must be leaping about to make all that noise. He remembered how he had once done that himself, a long time ago but not as far back as woolly mammoth time because yo yitsoo did not go that far back. They didn't go very far back at all though it did feel like that. Grandpa Yo Yitsoo shook his head. No, he wasn't nearly as old as he felt. He couldn't be because that girl Lucy had invented him.

'She invented me,' sighed Grandpa Yo Yitsoo, 'and she made me old and she made me feel that I was around before she invented me. I feel like I have hundreds of years in my pocket but I was only invented last Tuesday. That's magic and magic can do anything and sucks to you.' Grandpa Yo Yitsoo kicked a chair by the table, then he kicked the table, then he took as many

140

books off the shelf as he could hold and threw them on the floor.

'I hate magic,' shouted Grandpa Yo Yitsoo. 'It isn't fair. It just isn't fair that I was invented last Tuesday and those trolls have been around more or less since the beginning of time. No wonder they're so proud, so garumscoly bolly proud and put their tails in the air whenever they can get away with it. I hate trolls because it just ain't fair.'

Slowly Grandpa Yo Yitsoo made his way up the stairs. The noise was growing louder and louder. He thought he could feel something on his shoulder and tried to brush it away. Must be a spider. His fingers explored his neck and his shoulders but whatever it was had gone. 'I hate trolls,' whispered Grandpa Yo Yitsoo opening the trap door.

They were all dancing and singing. That blue moon must have sent them mad. Fireworks were going off in all directions. They were whizzing and banging and spreading stars all over the deck and the sky. A whirlwind of fireworks had engulfed the ship and the trolls had gone crazy with excitement. Yes, there he was, Lucy's dad, him with the twenty-six reasons bouncing up and down and clapping his hands.

'I'm no longer a pelican,' he was shouting.

'Someone remembered the twenty-six reasons —and very good reasons too, though I will admit that trolls do exist!'

'Some fool,' thought Grandpa Yo Yitsoo. 'Some fool remembered those twenty-six reasons. I wish you were back in that cage and a pelican. Now we'll never hear the end of it.'

Something had landed on his head. Something with wings. Carefully Grandpa Yo Yitsoo folded his fingers round the bat and held it up to his face.

'What do you want to tell me?'

'Your fault,' said the bat. 'All your fault. You were the one who stupidly remembered the twenty-six reasons and said them out loud.'

Grandpa Yo Yitsoo closed his eyes remembering. That was the problem with magic. You never knew where you were with it. You did something silly and it all came undone and you couldn't put it back together again. Now Lucy's dad was out of the cage and no longer a pelican fox and there was nothing to be done.

'It's getting worse,' whispered the bat. 'Much worse.'

'What do you mean,' shouted Grandpa Yo Yitsoo. 'It couldn't get any worser. It just couldn't, not even in a blue moon.'

'Oh, yes,' said the bat. 'Now the fun is going to begin. Just look over there.'

'Over where?'

'There!'

'There, where?'

'Up there, close to top of the mast, standing on top of the lookout post. She is tiny, ever so tiny but look and you can see her. '

'Why, it's Lucy!'

'Of course it's Lucy.'

'How did she get there?'

'Some bat took here there. Some bat who likes her, some friend of Henrietta the witch or Fiendish, or that dog Tickles. Someone from that crew. First she was in your pocket, then in your hat, then on your shoulders, then back in your pocket, and all the time she was listening.'

'Then she knows how to uninvent,' shuddered Grandpa Yo Yitsoo.

Just then a shadow fell and everyone was silent. Grandma Yo Yitsoo was back. She took Lucy in one of her huge hands and whispered something in her ear. The whisper was like a strong wind but no one could make out what she was saying. Then she put Lucy back. Lucy lifted her hands to show everyone that she was about to speak and the big blue moon slid across the sky till it was just above her, shedding a bowl of blue light on the mast. Although she was very small, they could all see her in the blue light and the more they looked, the bigger she seemed to grow till she was nearly her own old size. Henry couldn't stop looking. Fiendish and Henrietta the witch were standing right next to Henry, their eyes on Lucy. They noticed that there was someone else up there too. Yes, it was the troll, the little troll, but he too seemed bigger. The only sound they could hear was the sound of the wind in the woods and Lucy's dad's voice. 'I know that trolls do exist,' he was saying. 'And now I can even think of twenty-six reasons why.'

'Shut up!' shouted Grandpa Yo Yitsoo and he stamped and everyone stamped to show that they agreed with him. Then they waited for Lucy to say something.

'Rim ram rum, fire and snow, ice and sun by the magic that's begun, let night and air dissolve whoever I name. Let them be gone. Rim ram rum.'

She waved at everyone below.

'Go on,' said Grandma Yo Yitsoo. 'You just go on, you silly girl. But if you're not careful, you'll never change size!'

'Every yo yitsoo that ever wanted to eat a troll.'

'That's not me,' whispered Grandma Yo Yitsoo.

'Not me,' whispered Grandpa Yo Yitsoo. 'I never ever wanted a troll for breakfast. Disgusting thing to eat.'

'Rim, ram, rum fire and snow, ice and sun by the magic that's begun, let night and air dissolve every garingay. Let them be gone. Rim ram rum.'

She lifted her hands and the troll clapped. The blue moon was nodding and along the deck blew a wind; a strong mighty wind and they could feel something being blown away.

'Rim, ram rum!' shouted Lucy.

A cloud of bats rose into the air and sailed across the blue moon. One minute their black shapes danced across its surface, the next a fresh blast of wind came out of the wood chasing a dark mass of cloud that made the moon disappear. Henry looked up at the mast but he couldn't see his sister anywhere and all around him was a strange, solid darkness.

9

Back Home

'Everyone laughs at me at work.'

They were all in the garden. Lucy and Henry were lying on the grass while their mum and dad were sitting at a small wooden table.

'I tell them that there's a wood behind our garden and that it is full of magic, but no one listens. I explain to them that it's not as bad as it was because there are only trolls there now. Trolls, a few witches, a creature called Fiendish and Grandpa and Grandma Yo Yitsoo, but they're all right. They understand humans really, they are kind of human themselves and anyhow Lucy couldn't uninvent them because then she would have stayed small. She needed Grandma Yo Yitsoo to give her some cakes that do the opposite of the other cakes, the ones that make you small. I have explained that to people over and over again, but they don't listen. I tell them that there are lots of reasons why they should listen to me, but they just laugh. Well, one day they'll be sorry. They'll be really sorry because the world is full of trolls and you ought to be prepared so you know just what to do when all the magic takes off. If you don't, then you might just end up a pelican fox and in a cage. And if the moon happens to be blue then there is no end to what might happen. No end at all.' He looked thoughtfully at the wood. 'I can think of at least twenty-six reasons why people should beware of trolls but I'll keep them all to myself because people go around saying I am mad. Mad! They're mad. People who don't believe in trolls are crazy.'

Henry and Lucy let their dad talk. His voice drifted across the lawn. He didn't sound angry, just a bit confused. Why didn't people believe in trolls when he told them they were real? 'There's a troll,' he would say, 'a really small troll who likes to take his invisible dog for a walk in our garden. The dog is called Tickles. Next time you come round, I'll show you my troll.' But no one came round. People stayed away because they thought he was mad.

'I don't really mind that,' he way saying. 'Not

really. That means we can have our garden and our wood all to ourselves.'

Lucy and Henry looked at him and nodded. Yes, that was the best. This place was theirs, all theirs.

'Though someone could say,' continued their father stroking an invisible dog, 'that it isn't ours really, not at all.'

In his pocket Henry could feel the card the troll had given him. Guest Pass Magic Garden First Order, it said on it. Now they all three had one. The trees just stood there, stretching their branches as if they too might move any moment. The fence was sliding open and there was the troll.

'You'll never believe it,' he was saying. 'What they've all been up to. Trouble brewing. Why, Grandpa Yo Yitsoo and Fiendish…'

'Thought so,' interrupted their father making himself comfortable in his chair. 'Those two! Why, I can think of twenty-six reasons…'

Miranda Twist

Miranda grew up in Scotland. She studied
Archaeology and Anthropology at university.
She enjoys writing poems and short stories.
Once in a Blue Moon is her first book for children.

Maxim's All Night Diner — Mikka Haugaard

A wicked box of stories about witches and trolls. Annabel is doing research on witches and she discovers that London is full of them, as is New York. The world of magic is never far away.

'Fine rumbustious story telling.'
Jill Paton Walsh, winner of the Smarties Prize

£7.99 Paperback illustrated 208 pages ISBN 978-1-911427-00-1

Dylan and the Deadly Dimension—Mark Bardwell

When Dylan Thompson discovers a snake under the plughole in his bathroom, life takes a peculiar turn in this gripping fantasy adventure. After the death of his mother, Dylan escapes into a world of books. One day he discovers a sinister bookshop and a bookseller intent on doing dark things with words and fiction. Using fiction, someone has created the Deadly Dimension which is devouring the real world. Dylan meets Rollovkarghjicznilegogoh-Vylopophyngh (Rollo for short), a being from another reality, a well meaning but unreliable friend and guide in a new and dangerous world.

'Offers nifty worldbuilding and creative ideas in a fast-paced adventure.'
Kirkus Reviews.

Longlisted for the Pan MacMillan Write Now Prize.

£7.99 Paperback 208 pages   ISBN 978-1-911427-03-2